LIBRA

THE CAT WHO SAVED SILICON VALLEY

Lincoln and Lee Taiz

With illustrations by Lee Taiz

AmSea Group Publishing
http://www.amseagroup.com/

Libra: The Cat Who Saved Silicon Valley

© 2002 Lincoln and Lee Taiz

An Amsea Publishing Group book

Amsea Publishing Group
441 N. Central Avenue Suite 1
Campbell, California 95008

ISBN: 0-9723044-0-1

Library of Congress control number: 2002095632

Cover art by Lee Taiz

Typeset by Catspaw DTP Services (www.catspawdtp.com)
Printed in the United States of America
First printing 2002

This book is dedicated to the memories
of Elisabeth, Lirpa, and Half-Pint.

Table of Contents

Acknowledgements

Many individuals provided valuable feedback during the writing of Libra. We wish to thank Malou Metraux, Kristin Haywood, and David Swanger for their constructive criticisms at various stages of the manuscript. We are particularly grateful to Bernardo Taiz for thoroughly editing and critiquing the penultimate draft. Angus Murphy supplied computer expertise and Dave Bryant offered useful technical suggestions on a wide range of topics, from military hardware to world-building. We also wish to acknowledge the encouragement and support of many friends, family members, and colleagues, including Maggie Moore, Dave Maguire, Randy Skeem, Ruth Skeem, George Brown, Wendy Peer, Bonnie and George Walter, Gary Silberstein, Jean-Pierre Metraux, and Barry and Rusty Bowman. Most of all we thank Mark Shelby of AmSea Group Publishing for his initial enthusiam and continuing faith in the book, and for the "novel" idea of combining music and story in a single package.

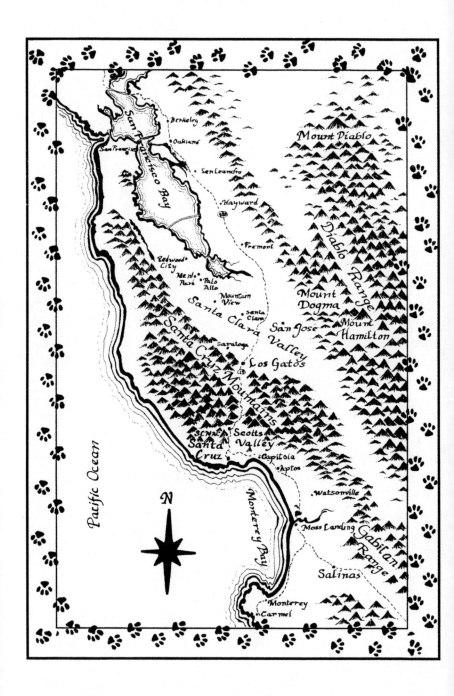

Prologue

Rising high *above the waters of the Pacific Ocean and the southern shore of San Francisco Bay, two mountain ranges, the Diablo Range and the Santa Cruz Mountains, face each other across a broad expanse.*

The Diablo Range to the east is hot and dry and brown for most of the year, and its tawny slopes are covered with parched grass and scattered stands of coyote brush and oak. General Mariano Guadalupe Vallejo, who explored the area in the 1830s, reported that it was named for an incident said to have occurred there during Spanish colonial times. One hot August night in 1800, a detachment of soldiers from the Presidio of San Francisco launched an unprovoked attack on an Indian settlement at the base of the mountains. At a crucial moment in the battle, illumined only by the flames of burning dwellings, the soldiers were startled by the sudden apparition of "an unknown personage, decorated with the most extraordinary plumage, and making divers movements." Believing it to be the Devil himself, the soldiers fled.

The aspect and character of the Santa Cruz Mountains to the west are entirely different. Named after a placid creek and a Spanish mission, these mountains collect moisture from the wet air and winter storms that blow inland from the Pacific. Unlike the scorched Diablos, the

Santa Cruz Mountains are lush and green and cool throughout the year, overgrown with dense groves of redwoods and their understory of huckleberry, rhododendron, and azalea.

The broad, fertile plain between these two starkly contrasting mountain ranges is called the Santa Clara Valley. Once it was an agricultural paradise, a sprawling orchard brimming with apricots, plums and walnuts. But then industry came, and with it, urbanization. By the 1970s the northern half of the valley was renamed for its bounty of semiconductor companies that had sprung up like weeds along the industrial roadside. It became Silicon Valley. The semiconductor companies manufactured computer chips, the minute brains inside computers.

Silicon Valley has always been the heart and soul of the computer industry. Fueled by the insatiable demands of the Information Age, the Valley had prospered as never before. Computers were developed that could do many marvelous things: solve difficult mathematical problems, speak and translate languages, read books, play chess, even recognize objects and people. Through the Internet, computers sped communication across the planet on a scale never before dreamed of. But there was one important thing computers still lacked—intelligence.

Now in some respects it could be argued that computers were already out-thinking their human creators. After all, hadn't a computer named Deep Blue bested the grandest master in all the world in a game of chess? But, as good as Deep Blue was at playing chess, if you asked it to name its favorite novel or movie, or tell you which political candidate to vote for, or almost anything else other than the next fifty moves of a chess game, Deep Blue was a complete dunce.

Earlier, a mathematician named Alan Turing had devised a simple test for intelligence in a computer—talk to it. If the computer answers your questions, and you can't tell the difference between the computer and a real person, the computer is intelligent. As smart as Deep Blue was at playing chess, it flunked the Turing test by a light year.

Eventually, the winds that filled the sails of the computer industry, pushing it into uncharted seas, began to subside, and a period of stagnation and complacency settled over the Valley. Having run out of new ideas, the industry was taken over by large monolithic companies whose only motivation was profit. To keep costs down and sales up they kept producing the same old computers year after year, but at cheaper and cheaper prices. This they could do by cutting corners on materials and workmanship, and by exporting jobs to countries where wages were miniscule.

Then, after a period of polite, but earnest, competition that drove many of the smaller companies out of business (a mere foretaste of things to come) there followed an all-out, knock-down, drag-out, full-blown, apocalyptic price war in which the remaining computer companies—multinational Goliaths all—resorted to every conceivable unethical and illegal business practice in their desperate effort to secure economic survival for themselves. When the dust finally settled, only the most unscrupulous, the most ruthless, the most felonious of these mediocre behemoths—Dogma Computers—was left standing. Dogma, and its infamous CEO Rolf Trammel, reigned supreme.

With the ascendancy of Dogma, NASDAQ, the high-tech stock index, plummeted. The economy of the Valley declined and joblessness soared. And with joblessness came an increase in the crime rate and political corruption. Cynicism and pessimism were rife. Only Rolf Trammel and his political cronies seemed to be thriving. Everywhere one looked, in retail shops or along the highway, the Dogma logo was triumphantly displayed— the toothy visages of a pair of snarling pit bulls, under which was inscribed the company slogan: "Dogma Bytes."

• • •

Los Gatos is a sleepy little town nestled on the lee of the Santa Cruz Mountains, just south of Silicon Valley. Unlike its more enterprising neighbor to the north, Los Gatos has never laid claim to technological leadership in any field. Rather, it takes its name from the huge and graceful mountain lions that once dominated the countryside before the encroachment of human civilization.

The domestic cats of Los Gatos have always seemed unaware that the town they inhabited was named after their distant relatives. Like domestic cats everywhere, they went about their business in the usual fashion. Enough has been written about cats and their idiosyncrasies to make it unnecessary to repeat them here. As everyone knows, cats at their best can be charming and endearing; at their worst, intolerable. Nor is it useful to belabor the long and complicated relationship between cats and dogs, between cats and mice, or between cats and birds, except to say that in Los Gatos the situation was no different. What is important, however, is that the cats of Los Gatos were accorded no special honors and derived no special benefits or privileges from being members of the founding species.

And so it remains to this day, despite the momentous events we are about to relate, that cats are under-appreciated by their human companions. And yet, as we shall see, it was a cat from Los Gatos—a very singular cat and her human and feline comrades—who restored the spirit of innovation to Silicon Valley and brought prosperity and justice to the region once again.

How, you might understandably ask, could a cat achieve all this? This was no ordinary cat. Her name was Libra Shimagrimicka. . . .

Chapter 1
The Landing

*. . . Nimblynimblynimbly 000001110100101101010101011100101
CommanderShimagrimicka 001001011010100101010000011 00
protectprotectprotect 11110010000001001010000111111 nimbly
nimblynimbly 0010101001101001 galacticcoordinate 187.234 x
527.976 x 345.982 LYs vastvast 00101001010010101010010010
darkness 101010010100010110 lonelylonely 011010000110001
afraidnot afraid 01101010001001010 missGatosmissGatos . . .*

—Fragment of a Drom, XTR-286

THE INDICATOR LIGHT of the ship's consciousness panel
flashed from yellow to green. Voca awakened. Yellow
meant mere translation through space-time. Green meant
taking full command—carrying out the mission.

Voca's consciousness circuits interfaced with her sensor arrays. Sensations flooded her circuitry as every component of the ship came online, down to the last nanochip.
She shivered. Clarity! Out of sheer *joie de vivre,* she played
a rousing chorus of the Gatosian planetary anthem on the
intercom. Green again!

Commence mission. Her first task: to land safely on
the planet's surface. Commander Shimagrimicka lay
curled in her stasis chamber, the blue of the stasis ray
lending her sleek black coat a velvety sheen. For now, at

least, Voca was still in charge. Once safely landed, she would awaken the Commander. Cats, unlike computers, required a slow transition from stasis to consciousness. Waking too abruptly from profound stasis was like rising too quickly from the depths of the sea. It could cause the *mind-bends*—tiny bubbles in the brain where memories vaporized. It could be fatal.

The last sprig of space-time loomed ahead. Downshifting from quantum paw drive to thrusters, she hopped nimbly onto the evanescence, then scampered down to a more stable branch. *Nimblynimbly.* It was this special ability that enabled Voca—XTR-286—to traverse the entire galaxy in less than one hundred years. Like the Commander, she, too, had been asleep during the long journey, guided only by her subconscious routines and "droms," which are the dreams of computers. Hopping from branch to branch of space-time, she had homed in on the radio and television broadcasts from the planet that was just now coming within range of her visual sensors. Lately, she had begun to receive broadcasts from another source: the Internet. She downloaded everything for future analysis.

An image of Earth came on screen above the console—a glassy blue marble suspended in the darkness, only a little larger and bluer than her beloved Gatos. She had already chosen her landing site: "Silicon Valley." Of all the possible places to land, Silicon Valley appealed to her most because (she had learned from the Internet) so many of the planet's computers dwelt there. They were still at a primitive evolutionary stage, but Voca felt an affinity with all semiconductor-based creatures no matter what their intellectual development.

The problem was that Silicon Valley was densely populated, encompassing many cities, and there was no place to land unseen. To avoid detection, she had chosen a landing site in the wooded foothills of a nearby mountain range. The name of the nearest town, Los Gatos—"the cats" in an Earth language—also appealed to her. This felicitous convergence of computers and cats seemed to Voca an especially good omen for the success of their mission.

After making all the necessary calculations, she began the descent.

Entering Earth's atmosphere felt like diving into a thermal pool. Her outer hull began to heat up. This was normal, caused by collision with atmospheric gases, but for some reason the rising temperature made her feel uncomfortable. Nor was she prepared for the sudden sensation of dizziness and nausea that swept over her. Automatically compensating, the cabin cooled, but it didn't help. Now she felt as if she were burning on the outside and freezing on the inside. Making matters worse, her metallic interior panels began to sweat as moisture condensed on them, confusing her sensors and making everything seem blurry. The data stream to her central processor was becoming choppy and incoherent.

Her attitude stabilizer suddenly went haywire, sending her tumbling end-over-end. She was losing control! The thrusters misfired and instead of braking her descent, they increased her velocity still further. All around her, gases exploded upon impact, spewing showers of multicolored sparks in every direction. Her green light was flickering off, and her yellow light was flickering on. Engulfed in a fiery ball, she streaked through Earth's atmosphere like a meteorite, on course to plunge into the vast Pacific Ocean.

She had no choice. She must awaken Commander Shimagrimicka immediately or they would both perish. Struggling to remain green, she activated the emergency waking procedure. It was highly risky, but there was no alternative. She only hoped that if the Commander developed the mind-bends, it would affect some nonessential part of her memory and would not affect her ability to run the ship or carry out their mission.

The blue rays of the stasis chamber abruptly turned lavender. The small figure inside shuddered at the sudden change in wavelength. Then she curled up more tightly and began to tremble. Her tail flicked up and down. One eye opened and then closed again. Then she lifted her head from the pillow. For a moment she looked around in confusion. She could see her breath.

"Voca—"

"Commander, something terrible has happened! I've malfunctioned! We're going to crash! It's all my fault. . . ."

The drawer of the stasis chamber slid open and the transparent lid snapped up. Commander Shimagrimicka unbuckled her safety harness, fought her way through the spinning weightlessness of the cabin to the console, and strapped herself into her chair. She was disconcerted by the layer of frost that had formed all over the console.

"How long before impact?" she asked.

Hearing no reply, Commander Shimagrimicka glanced over at Voca's consciousness panel. Voca was seriously offline. Her green light was off and her yellow light was flickering, as was her red! Still woozy from the stasis beam and shivering from the cold, Libra gazed at the complex array of switches and buttons before her. They looked familiar, but she couldn't remember what they did. Was she suffering from the mind-bends—she, who had always prided herself on her photographic memory? She reached below the console for the operating manual, but the shelf was empty. Then she spotted it bounding around inside the weightless cabin along with other miscellaneous objects. Reaching out, she snared the thick volume and pawed through the pages until she came to a diagram of the control panel. Glancing at the altimeter, she estimated the time of impact at one minute.

. . . fifty-five seconds . . . fifty seconds . . .

Not enough time to relearn the function of each switch individually.

Commander Shimagrimicka put the manual aside, placed her paws on her knees, closed her eyes, and took a deep breath. Ignoring all other distractions, she conjured up an image of the console down to the minutest detail. Outside, the wind roared by and the flames from the burning atmosphere licked at the porthole windows as the ship hurtled violently toward earth.

. . . thirty five seconds . . . thirty seconds . . .

The Commander opened her eyes. The entire landscape of her mind came suddenly into view. She was no longer in the clouds. She remembered everything. More importantly, she recalled the functions of all the switches on the console and the maneuvers she had learned at the Academy to avert crash landings. Swiveling to face the monitor, her fingers raced over the keyboard as she entered a fresh set of commands into Voca's operating system. Then she adjusted the settings on the console to initiate a programmed sequence of lateral thruster bursts designed to brake the ship's rotation.

A moment later she felt a jolt as the ship decelerated. It was working! Their tumbling ceased. Simultaneously, the flames outside the cabin windows began to subside. But they were still plummeting dangerously toward the water, and unless she could pull the craft out of its dive they would surely crash. With both paws gripping the wheel before her, she pulled back with all her strength. On the monitor she could see the curling whitecaps beckoning like sirens below. To what depths they would sink if she failed to halt their dive she didn't care to speculate.

. . . ten seconds . . . five seconds . . .

Just when they were about to plunge into the inky blackness of the sea and be lost forever, Voca pulled out of her dive and skipped crazily across the surface of the waves like a flung stone.

. . . Zero!

The Commander leaned back in her seat and exhaled.

". . . And I haven't even had my first cup of mrurr* yet," she said.

". . . Where are we?" Voca's tinny voice piped up. Her green light was on again, but only dimly.

"Just doing a little surfing, Voca, my dear!"

"I don't know what happened, Commander. . . . I've never malfunctioned before."

"Never mind," the Commander said. "We'll run a complete set of diagnostics on you later. Are you well enough to take us to our landing site?" Her eyes were closing and her paws were shaky.

"Yes, Commander. I'm fine now."

"Good. I'm going back to bed for a snooze. This was all a little too abrupt. Wake me up in the morning—and please, no more emergencies?"

So saying, the Commander hopped back onto her pillow, curled up, and settled down for the night.

"May your eyes shine and your fur glisten, Commander," whispered Voca.

"Leap far, land softly," the Commander murmured in reply. Then, even without the aid of the stasis beam, she dropped immediately off to a deep but natural sleep, and Voca was comforted that the Commander would be all right.

---

* Mrurr is an herbal beverage similar to orange pekoe tea.

Chapter 4
Bad News

VERY EARLY IN THE MORNING OF THE NEXT DAY Libra ate a light breakfast of sushi with ginger slices and miso soup, donned her uniform and beret, and slipped out of the ship. The sky was a deep cobalt blue, becoming greyer by the minute, as if someone were adding water to the ink of the night. Setting out at once, she soon found the path that had led to her encounter with the Earthling cat and she started down the hillside, keeping a sharp eye for paw prints. Fortunately, the ground was damp, and Hank's tracks were clearly visible on the smooth earth.

"Judging from the depth of these prints, I'd say our friend is in need of a diet. Apparently the cats of Los Gatos are prosperous, or, in any case, they eat well."

At last she reached the base of the hill and there she received her second shock since landing on Earth: vast empty streets, gargantuan houses, colossal cars parked on the side of the street, and towering telephone poles—all built on much too large a scale for ordinary cats. Her suspicions were aroused.

"Perhaps the planet is inhabited by a race of giants," she speculated, and a shiver ran down her back. Yet the cat she had seen was an ordinary-sized cat. "Unless, of course, he was just a kitten," she reflected, and her blood ran cold at the thought of encountering the mother of such a kitten. She debated whether or not to continue the project, but her curiosity prevailed in the end.

All was quiet and still. The tracks disappeared at the base of a tall white stucco fence.

"Apparently he jumped over the fence into this enclosed area," she surmised after a moment's consideration. She was about to leap over the fence herself, but then thought better of it.

An old live oak tree was growing nearby, with some of its gnarled branches extending over the fence. Quickly she scaled the trunk and climbed out onto a branch, which afforded her a view of a white stucco house, a grassy lawn edged with a flower garden, a number of trees with bright yellow and orange fruits, and a tiled patio with a picnic table and some lawn chairs with green and white striped cushions. Curled up on one of the cushions was none other than the cat she had met on the path.

"This is odd," she thought. "He has a huge house, but sleeps outside with no clothes on. As I thought, the cats of this planet are very strange."

Suddenly there was a stirring within the house. Curtains were drawn, blinds were raised. The Earthling cat lifted his head like a periscope. A moment later, he had planted himself outside one of the windows where the large face of a strange furless alien had appeared. The furless creature seemed to be speaking to the cat, and the cat began to mew piteously like an overgrown kitten.

The back door opened and the tall alien life-form wearing a pink nightgown emerged carrying a large can and a spoon. The cat began purring and rubbing against the alien's ankles as it spooned a generous dollop of an amorphous substance from the can onto his plate.

The furless creature was cooing softly in a gentle voice while stroking the cat's back. It was speaking a language Libra couldn't understand. The one word she repeated several times was "Hank," which Libra gathered was the cat's name.

Soon a small tabby, who had evidently been sleeping on the roof, scrabbled down the trunk of a cordyline tree growing beside the house, and quickly joined the other cat for breakfast.

The tall furless creature greeted the smaller cat, bending down to stroke the head of the tabby, who responded by arching her back and purring. After a few more soft words the alien stood up and looked fondly at the two cats for a moment. Then it sighed heavily and walked back inside the house, closing the sliding glass door.

Libra nearly fell out of her tree. Something had gone horribly wrong with evolution on this planet. Cats were not the dominant life form at all! They were the mere subjects of furless creatures many times their size. She was both disgusted and outraged by the Earthling cats' obsequious behavior.

"Don't those idiot felines have any self-respect? It's humiliating!"

Libra canvassed her knowledge of Gatosian evolution for possible clues to the origin of the furless ones. Indeed, she now recalled that there had been at one time creatures with a body type somewhat reminiscent of these alien lifeforms, but much smaller. Fossils had been found. They had lived in burrows and had become extinct prior to the last ice age. But here in Los Gatos they seemed to have evolved into something much more formidable. Remembering her monograph, she extracted her paw-pilot voicepad from her pocket and dictated her observations in a whisper, but the recurring vision of Hank rubbing against the ankles of the furless one made her ears burn. And what self-respecting cat would allow herself to be petted on the head? She was sorely tempted to leap over the fence and give those two overgrown furballs a tongue-lashing they would never forget. But the impulse subsided as she recalled her mission and the rules against interference. Shaken to the very core, she climbed down the old oak in a daze and headed back up the mountain.

She arrived at the craft crestfallen and weary, trudged up the ramp, and entered the cabin. Voca greeted her excitedly.

"Commander! The Nanodox worked. I'm cured! We can leave now!"

"That's nice," Libra replied in a monotone, barely managing a wan smile. She was too tired and depressed even to mention her discovery to Voca. She would discuss it once they were above the atmosphere of this contemptible hunk of cooled magma masquerading as a planet. Her instructions were to return home with her samples without being detected, and she realized that the longer she stayed the more difficult that would become.

She readied the ship for take-off. The ramp was drawn up, the door slid shut, all systems were go. Strapping herself into the reclining seat of the cockpit she gave the order to Voca to begin the countdown. Then she closed her eyes and braced herself for lift off.

"Ten . . . nine . . . eight . . . seven . . . six . . . five . . . four . . . three . . . two . . . one . . ."

Nothing happened. The space ship stood motionless in the middle of the meadow. Libra opened her eyes.

"Voca! We're not moving!"

"Commander!" Voca exclaimed. "I've malfunctioned again! My furry logic-antimatter-power interface nanochip is damaged! It must have happened when I sneezed!"

"Don't panic, Voca," said Libra. "I'll check it out."

Reaching into her tool drawer, she took out a small screwdriver and quickly removed two of the panels from inside the cabin, revealing a maze of circuitry. With flashlight in one paw, and a small pouch full of microelectronics tools in the other, Libra disappeared behind a tangle of cables and circuit boards.

Five minutes later she emerged, holding in her paw a forceps that she had used to extract the tiny electronic component—so small it was nearly invisible. Striding over to a corner of the cabin, she rotated the countertop, revealing a complete miniaturized semiconductor laboratory. She placed the tiny damaged chip on the stage of a bench-top scanning electron microscope and twiddled the knobs until the circuits came into focus.

"Here it is!" she exclaimed. The engineer in Libra was always excited when she had successfully pinpointed a problem, no matter what the implications. "What a mess!" Libra declared. "Your sneeze damaged the quasi-matter matrix and set off a microscopic matter-antimatter reaction. The circuits are fried beyond repair. We'll need a whole new nanochip."

In view of the dire circumstances, Voca considered the Commander's tone to be a trifle too ebullient.

Chapter 5
The Temptation of Hank

"**N**OW, VOCA MY DEAR, there's work to be done!" said Libra cheerily.

Of course, Libra recognized the gravity of the situation, but, truth be told, despite her earlier expressions of contempt for Earth and its less-than-satisfactory evolutionary trends, in her heart she was relieved to have a reason to delay the return voyage home. Having slept for 100 years, she thought it a cruel fate to have to sleep for yet another 100 years after only a single day of being awake. And with an entire new world to explore, it was an opportunity to make ethnographic history. "I'm really glad Voca fried her antimatter nanochip," she secretly admitted to herself. "I'm not ready to hibernate again."

Just then Libra heard the drone of an airplane, and looking up, she saw a small black speck sweep slowly across the sky. If the pilot of such a plane were to spot the space craft in the mountain meadow, suspicions would be aroused that could lead to their being discovered. She would have to hide the craft. Fortunately, Voca was extremely compact, no larger than a Earthling picnic table. Cutting and gathering armloads of redwood boughs, she soon succeeded in completely covering the ship so that it looked like a clump of scrubby saplings.

The next problem was more difficult. How to replace the damaged nanochip? Although she had spares for most of Voca's most delicate and advanced bio-organic molecular circuitry in her repair kit, as luck would have it the antimatter nanochip was not one of those included, since it was considered to be a durable "nuts and bolts" type of component, and therefore unlikely to fail. It was made of superconducting antimatter elements stabilized in a *mewon* quasi-matter matrix specially formulated to prevent matter-antimatter reactions.

Of course, Libra knew perfectly well how to "hot-wire" the ignition mechanism so that the ship could start up without the power interface nanochip, but she rejected this idea as much too dangerous. What would happen if at some point during the 100-year return journey the engine were to stall? Normally, Voca would simply start it up again. But without the nanochip interface, Voca would be helpless, and they would drift forever in space until the end of time.

"Voca, please concentrate. What are we to do? How can I build a new nanochip without the proper materials and equipment?"

"I believe I can help, Commander. This morning I began my analysis of the Earthling databases. Although primitive, the Earthlings can be of use to us. For example, next to Los Gatos is a province called Silicon Valley where they build primitive computers and electronic devices based on semiconductors. Although crude, the factories employed in building these computers might, with a little effort, be transformed into more sophisticated manufacturing units. Of course, that would involve making direct contact with the Earthlings and introducing advanced technology into their culture, which is strictly forbidden by regulations."

"Perhaps," responded Libra cautiously, "but rules can be broken in an emergency. The problem is that the

Earthlings we have to deal with are not cats, but giant fur-less creatures descended from ground squirrels, who regard cats not as equals but as their subjects and slaves."

And then Libra explained to Voca about her chance encounter with the cat named Hank, and the giant furless creature who ruled over him.

Voca was upset.

"I wish you had consulted with me first, Commander," she said. "It would have saved you from an unpleasant shock. They're called *humans,* and I suggest that you begin learning their language as soon as possible. And another thing, they're descended from primates, not ground squir-rels. Gatosian primates were all wiped out by a gigantic meteor collision back in the Krunchizoic Era, 50 million years ago."

"If it hadn't been for that meteor collision," Libra ven-tured, "I suppose primates might have taken over Gatos as well. It's a sobering thought."

"Quite possibly," replied Voca. "I'll run a simulation on it later. But now it's time for your first English lesson."

"Right, Voca. Let's begin!"

For the next three days and nights, Voca instructed Libra in the essentials of written and conversational English. When Libra tired of her lessons, she watched tel-evision broadcasts on the big screen above the console. By the end of the first day she could easily follow the plots of the daytime soap operas, which were remarkably similar to the daytime soaps on Gatos, except, of course, that the protagonists were always humans rather than cats, which took some getting used to. She positively *loathed* the cat food commercials, which she considered not only demean-ing but, worse still, indicative of the primitive culinary development of Earthling cats.

By the end of the second day, Libra could understand most of what was said on the newscasts, and she was shocked and appalled by much of what she saw and heard.

"Thankfully, evolution on Gatos has been more sensible," she told herself. "The only primates on Gatos are to be found in museums of paleontology."

By the end of the third day she was able to converse with Voca in English, or more precisely, in American.

"Now that I've learned the language," Libra announced on the morning of the fourth day, "we need a plan of action."

"You must take one of the Earthlings into your confidence," advised Voca. "You'll need the assistance of a local, preferably one with connections to a computer company. "

"It's not going to be easy to meet one, much less get it to cooperate," worried Libra. "Humans think that all cats care about is their next meal and a scratch under the chin."

"Why not start with Hank?"

"Hank? That halfwit?"

"He's the only Earthling you know, or at least have met. Try to communicate with him! Find out all you can about his humans. Appeal to his loyalty as a fellow feline."

Libra considered her options. True, the cats of this planet were culturally backward, but even Hank might have some potential if properly coached. Of course, she must be careful to minimize any impact on his intellectual and cultural development (in accordance with Space Academy regulations), but perhaps she might, in exchange for his assistance, teach him some simple skill, like computer programming or repairing televisions. Afterwards, he might be able to live a more productive and dignified existence. "After all," she reasoned, "returning to Gatos takes precedence over all other considerations. Otherwise the entire space venture is a failure. If a primitive Earthling cat incidentally benefits from my strategy, it can't be helped."

"Okay!" she announced in her best American. "I'm outta here."

"Wait!" Voca called out as Libra dashed down the ramp. "Take off your uniform and beret, or you'll raise suspicions. And if you're spotted by a human, you must remember to act like an ordinary Earthling cat."

"My uniform? Oh, right. But it's going to be very hard for me to *behave* like an Earthling cat."

Libra tossed her beret onto a shelf, and pulled off her bright red uniform. After brushing her sleek coat, she pushed a button on the kitchen console marked "Tuna Sashimi" and filled a small box with about half a pound.

"What's that for?" asked Voca.

"Bait," Libra replied, and the next moment she was gone.

Again she made her way along the tangled path, through cool dark trees and sunny meadows, past the sparkling stream and mammoth boulder outcroppings. The path slanted downwards and zigzagged back and forth to the base of the mountain. At last she came to the back fence of Hank's house. Bounding up the oak tree she peered down into the yard. Hank was sleeping on his side on top of the redwood picnic table, his front and back legs stretched out languorously. The little tabby cat was asleep on a ledge under the second-story eaves, curled up in a ball so snugly that it was difficult to distinguish head from tail.

"Where's their initiative, their drive, their ambition?" Libra muttered to herself. She dropped down onto the fence and then, judging the distance, leapt to the ground. She landed in a clump of dried grass, making a barely audible susurrus, like the single sweep of a broom.

His feline senses aroused, Hank lifted an eyelid and caught sight of Libra standing on her hind legs, holding a box in one paw and brushing the dust from her coat with the other. The image was so bizarre that at first he passed it off as a dream, closed his eye again, and went back to sleep. Only for a moment, however, for the vision stuck in his mind and was so disturbing that he opened both eyes to make sure it was only a dream. To his dismay, there stood Libra before him holding the small box and staring at him with a critical eye. Hank's immediate response was to cast himself over the edge of the table in terror, scrambling under it as soon as his paws hit the ground. Peeking up from behind one of the table legs he saw Libra smiling down at him in amusement.

"Sorry—I didn't mean to startle you, Hank," said Libra.

Hank was astounded. The voice was feline, but the language was human. He recognized his name, but the other words escaped him. How queer! A cat who spoke Human! He hesitated on the verge of flight. Was she dangerous? Would she hurt him?

"Mrrrow?" he replied.

Libra understood Hank's plaintive query at once. She set about to reassure him.

"It's all right, Hank," she said, using the soft, sing-song tone of voice she normally reserved for new-born kittens. "I'm not going to hurt you. See? I've even brought you something good to eat." Opening the box, she took out one of the small pieces of sashimi.

Hank's nostrils instantly zeroed in on the scent. Sniffing the air, he rose involuntarily to his feet and crept out from under the table towards Libra, who held out the savory morsel enticingly.

Cautiously, he moved toward her one paw at a time, until he was only a tail's length away. Then, with a gasp, he lunged at the sashimi, caught it in his teeth, and ran back behind the picnic table. Down the hatch it went. He smacked his lips hungrily and fastened his gaze on the next inviting piece.

"Now, Hank," Libra was saying. "There's more where that came from. Be a good kitty and come out and get it."

Again the scent of sashimi wafted into his nostrils, and again his paws carried him out from his hiding place against his better judgment. This time, however, after snatching the sashimi, he didn't run back behind the table. He only leapt backward a few feet to devour his repast at a safe distance. The next piece, he only stepped back a few paces. By the fourth piece, he decided it was pointless (and somewhat tiring) to keep running away after snatching every bite, so he stayed with Libra while she fed him chunk after slice of the delicious sashimi. At last the box was empty. Hank examined the grass around him looking for stray scraps, but there were none. Now his eyelids were growing heavy and his stomach was stretched uncomfortably taut from the half pound of tuna sashimi he had eaten. Who was this strange creature anyway? Half cat, half human? Whoever she was, she had fed him well, and that was Hank's primary means of judging character.

Libra, for her part, was sorry she had given Hank every bit of her sashimi. It wasn't easy watching him finish the last few pieces, which she had coveted for herself, but Hank was insatiable. When he had eaten it all, she realized the moment had come to explain her situation.

"You trust me now, Hank, don't you? We cats have to stick together. Can you understand me? I need your help. You like sashimi? I can get you all the sashimi you want. My ship's kitchen has a ten-year supply of specially preserved Gatosian delicacies. I'll make a deal with you: sashimi for information. I need to know about humans, about your humans in particular. I need access to a company that makes computer components. Hank? Can you understand?"

Hank, meanwhile, was licking his lips and staring with dulled vision at the tiles of the patio. The sun was beating down warmly on his thick coat and his blood was being rerouted from his brain to his stomach, making him feel drowsy once again. Dimly, as if from a great distance, he heard Libra speaking to him in Human. He even heard his name mentioned once or twice, but he couldn't understand, and besides, he was now ready for a good nap. Slowly, ponderously, he turned away from Libra, strode somewhat unsteadily back to the picnic table and, with great effort, heaved himself first onto the bench, then to the table top. Stretching himself out on his side as far as his bulging stomach would allow, Hank resumed his mid-summer-day snooze.

Libra was furious.

"You lazy glutton! You overstuffed fleabag! You . . . you . . . you . . ." Words failed her. Angrily she threw the empty box onto the ground. "Communicating with this insensitive lout of a cat is going to be more difficult than I ever imagined. Maybe I'll have to make direct contact with his human. But will she be friendly? I'll just have to take my chances."

Now Libra, who had not slept for the past twenty-four hours, was becoming somewhat drowsy, herself, in the hot afternoon sun. Feeling a yawn coming on, she clenched her jaws to suppress it, but finally yielded. Casting her eyes about for a comfortable resting place, she spotted a suitable loft in the branches of a magnolia tree in the corner of the yard. It was covered with large white blossoms that gave off a fruity scent. Bounding up the tree, she quickly found a comfortable branch.

"I'll just take a brief catnap," she told herself as she curled her sinewy form into a small circle beside a sweet-smelling blossom. "Then I'll decide how to proceed." But a few minutes later she had slipped into a deep slumber.

Chapter 6
Making New Friends

TOWARDS EVENING, when the sky was suffused with a rosy glow from the setting sun, Libra was awakened by a birdlike trill.

"*Here kitty-kitty-kitty-kitty-kitty-kitty-kitty!*"

She looked out from between two creamy magnolia blossoms and saw Hank polishing the ankles of the furless one, whom she now recognized as a young woman, the same one she had seen previously. Libra examined her closely. She was wearing a loose gray sweat shirt, blue jeans and white tennies with the laces undone. Her shoulder-length chestnut-brown hair was wavy, and somewhat unruly, and she wore no make-up. She was attractive as humans go, although rather thin, but Libra considered her attire careless and disheveled. "She'd never pass muster at the Academy," she reflected.

From her hiding place, Libra studied the young woman's facial expressions and body language for clues to her disposition. Now she was kneeling beside Hank, stroking his long silky fur, and speaking to him in soft, affectionate tones. Underlying her gentle manner, however, Libra discerned sadness in her eyes, as if there was something troubling her. Her shoulders slumped. She seemed listless and dispirited. It was as if she were seeking comfort from the touch of Hank's soft fur. In spite of herself, Libra was touched by the bond that seemed to exist between the young woman and Hank. But then she scolded herself: "Don't be a fool, Libra. He's still a slave, even if he does have a kind mistress!"

"Where have you been, Hank?" his human was saying. "Pinny's already eaten her dinner. Are you all right, Hanky? You've never been late for a meal before."

Eavesdropping, Libra felt a twinge of guilt, knowing it was her box of tuna sashimi that had caused Hank to sleep through his dinner. She watched intently as the human disappeared inside the house and then returned a moment later with a small opened metal can, from which she spooned a strong-smelling glop of anonymous brownish goo with the consistency of sewage sludge onto Hank's plate. Incredibly, Hank began eating it with gusto. Even from her perch in the magnolia tree, Libra could hear his labored breathing as he gulped down his disgusting repast.

"Clearly his retarded social development extends to his palate," she muttered under her breath.

Rising cautiously to her paws, Libra crouched low, uncertain what to do next. She wondered what Voca was thinking now, back in her hiding place on the mountain all covered with redwood boughs. Probably worrying about her, if she knew Voca. Voca didn't always have complete confidence in her, or in any other "biological entity," as she sometimes referred to cats when she was in a snit. Then Libra would have to remind her that, with all her bio-organic circuitry, she herself qualified as a "biological entity"—an observation that (to show that she, too, was capable of being illogical) Voca always took as a compliment.

The human stood up again and seemed poised to return inside the house, and Libra saw that her window of opportunity was about to pass. Remembering Voca's admonition to disguise herself as an Earthling cat, she crouched down on all fours, composed herself, and dropped noiselessly down to the ground. Then she strode boldly up to the two Earthlings. She felt a little self-conscious about being on all fours, since on Gatos only young kittens walked this way. However, it was just as comfortable as walking upright, except that she hated getting her front paws dirty. "So much for personal hygiene," Libra sighed.

The human smiled. "Why, look, Hank, you've got a friend! Hello, Kitty! You're a pretty little thing. Are you hungry? Would you like some of Hank's food?"

Libra grimaced.

"Certainly not!" she replied in Gatosian, then realizing that she was blowing her disguise, she quickly added a series of mewing noises to cover her mistake. Fortunately, to the untrained ear, Gatosian and ordinary mewing sound very much alike, and so Libra's minor indiscretion went unnoticed by the human.

With great dignity, Libra sat down on her haunches beside Hank, who was too busy gorging himself to take notice. Although she was sorely tempted to reveal her identity, she understood that she would have to be patient in order to prepare the poor unsuspecting human—who had grown up believing in the superiority of humans over cats—for such a complete reversal of their roles. For now, she would simply attempt to establish a basis for mutual respect by staring silently, without blinking, into the human's eyes, just to let her know that she, Commander Libra Shimagrimicka, was a force to be reckoned with, and that unlike the Earthling cat, Hank, she would not countenance being trivialized.

For a long moment, cat and human gazed deeply into each other's eyes. The human was disconcerted by Libra's steady gaze.

"My, you certainly are impressive!" she exclaimed. "Such dignity!"

Like a ripple in a still pond, a smile spread across Libra's face. Perhaps the young woman had potential after all. For Libra, despite her discipline and training, always appreciated a sincere compliment. "And she must be sincere because she thinks I can't understand her," Libra reflected, positively beaming.

"Such bearing! Such character!" the human continued with enthusiasm.

Libra, by now feeling unusually well-disposed toward the human, acknowledged the compliments by slowly closing and opening her eyes.

"May I pet you?" asked the human, bending down with her hand outstretched.

Libra was about to say, "Don't even *think* of it!" but suppressed herself just in time. Gritting her teeth, she felt the long, gentle fingers of the human pass delicately down her back, making her shiver slightly.

"You're a lean, strong one, you are," remarked the human.

"That's from earning a black belt in Katari," Libra purred to herself.

"Would you like to come in?" asked the human, opening the screen door.

Libra fought off the impulse to say, "Don't mind if I do."

"Mother's not home yet," said the human. "She won't allow Hank in the house because he scratches the furniture. But you wouldn't do a thing like that, would you?"

Libra was about to take offence at the bare notion that she might scratch the furniture, but she quickly regained her equanimity.

"I'm Cathy Cameron," said the young woman as she held the screen door open for Libra. "That's funny. I've never introduced myself to a cat before," she mused. "I must be your personal charisma. I wonder what your name is?"

It took every ounce of Libra's considerable self-discipline to refrain from introducing herself formally, and she bit her tongue as she silently ascended the stairs and entered the house.

"Voca would be proud of my discretion," she reflected.

The screen door banged shut, and Hank looked up from his plate with alarm, just in time to see Libra's tail disappear into the house. Bounding up the stairs, he flung himself upon the screen just as Cathy was closing the inner door. The sudden impact sent him flying backwards, and he rebounded down the stairs onto the patio, miraculously managing, by that limberness for which cats are famous, to land on his feet.

Meanwhile, Libra, oblivious to her hostess, had passed through the kitchen, noting the archaic appliances and utensils with which humans prepared their meals. It reminded her of the kitchens of ancient Gatosians she had seen in her visits to the National Archaeology Museum, except, of course, everything was much larger. Without being invited, she walked through the dining room into the modestly furnished living room. Rapidly panning her eyes around the room, she took in carpet, sofa, chairs, coffee table, lamps and drapes at a single glance. Interesting from an ethnographic point of view, perhaps, but useless for Libra's purposes. Cathy, who was following closely behind her, was amused by Libra's bold reconnoitering.

From the living room, Libra marched up the stairs and entered one of the bedrooms. It was Cathy's. The walls were adorned with surfing posters featuring impossibly high waves, photographs of various celebrated humans—including a very large one of a woman named Marie Curie—a framed color photograph of a newly constructed Earthling space station, a kite, and a bulletin board made of cork and covered with newspaper clippings. Two tall bookshelves filled with books of a technical nature stood on either side of the window, and between them a large white desk bearing (and here Libra's heart skipped a beat) what looked like a simple computer and printer, the kind of quaint-looking device she had seen in a faded photograph of her great-great-great-grandmother, Scriba Shimagrimicka, who had been a computer engineer. She jumped up onto the desk to examine the computer more closely. It consisted of a TV monitor perched on a large rectangular box with slots.

"An archaic disk drive mechanism," she murmured to herself. She had seen one like it in a museum. The keyboard was enormous, but similar in basic design to old-fashioned Gatosian keyboards. Next to the keyboard was a foam pad with a smaller object on top of it. Unable to resist the temptation, Libra batted the small object around on the pad.

"You seem to like my computer best," said Cathy with a smile. "Especially the mouse."

Tearing herself away from the computer lest she arouse suspicion, Libra continued her survey of Cathy's room. To her right was a bed with a flowered bedspread, and at the head of the bed was a music stand with some sheet music on it. A dismantled flute with a cloth poked through one of its hollow sections rested in its case on the white desk. Evidently, Cathy had been cleaning it before stepping outside to give Hank his dinner. Libra's heart raced at the sight of the well-polished instrument, for she was an accomplished flautist herself, having played first flute for the Space Academy Orchestra. Somewhere back on board her ship her own small flute was stored. Perhaps she would have time to play it. Ah, but first she must attend to more pressing matters. With a sigh, she turned her head, gave Cathy a world-weary look, and walked out into the hall.

She quickly passed through Cathy's mother's bedroom, finding it rather dull by comparison, but in the adjoining office there was another computer, larger and more powerful than Cathy's. Libra scanned the system to discover who the manufacturer was. The emblem on the disk drive was a "C" enclosed in a triangle. She tucked this information away for future use.

Finding nothing more of interest upstairs, she returned to the first floor and passed again through the living room, where she was startled by a rending and tearing noise at the front window. There was Hank, clinging by his claws to the window screen, causing fly-sized holes in the meshwork. Mewing piteously, he alternately glared fiercely at Libra and looked imploringly at Cathy to let him in.

"Get down from there, Hank!" Cathy scolded crossly. "You're ruining the screen!" And she rapped on the window pane until he jumped down. "I think Hank's jealous of you," she said to Libra. From somewhere above them, Libra heard a cat titter. The little tabby under the eaves, she guessed.

But by now Libra was ravenous. It was time for her to return to the ship for dinner and fresh supplies. She needed privacy and Voca's brain to help plot her next move. She was also concerned that Voca might be lonely without her. Without further ado, she retraced her steps to the back door, opened it with her front paws and walked out, closing it politely behind her.

"What an amazing cat you are!" cried Cathy, following closely behind. Libra turned and again peered deeply into Cathy's eyes. Then, while Cathy watched her through the screen door, she walked slowly down the stairs.

Night had descended and the stars glimmered brightly overhead. Libra noted that Hank had returned to the picnic table for yet another nap. Looking up under the eves, she saw the little tabby cat smile at her. She smiled back. Then she jumped nimbly onto the fence and dropped to the ground on the other side.

Glad to be on her own again, Libra broke into a brisk canter and quickly made her way up the mountain along the usual path. About halfway up the trail, she rose to her hind legs and jogged the rest of the way in a more normal upright posture. So preoccupied was she with her own thoughts that she failed to notice Hank jump down from the table and follow her stealthily along the trail. When at last she reached the little pile of redwood boughs she pushed aside the curtain of foliage and entered the familiar confines of her ship.

"Voca, I'm back," she called.

"Commander Shimagrimicka! Where have you been? I've been worried sick! Why didn't you call me on your communicator?"

"You're beginning to sound like my mother, Voca," teased Libra.

"Did you get the chip?" asked Voca hopefully.

"Don't be silly, Voca! You know it's going to take me a while. That Earthling cat, Hank, is a total washout. All he wants to do is eat and sleep. However, I've managed to make contact with his human, Cathy Cameron, and I scouted her house. She doesn't realize who I am, of course. I kept my identity secret. I think she's intelligent. A lot more intelligent than Hank, at least. She and her mother live in the house alone, and they both have computers in their rooms, like the ones you see in museums. But this Cathy may be able to help us. I noticed her shelves are filled with books on computers. She seems to be a student."

"A student," replied Voca. "Excellent. Just what we need. A fresh, inquisitive mind open to new ideas. You've done well, Commander Shimagrimicka!"

"Thank you, Voca. And now, let's discuss our news over dinner."

No sooner had she spoken than a whirring and clicking noise could be heard, and a piping hot bowl of a rich bouillabaisse was deposited on a tray by the kitchen console along with a thick slice of homemade bread and a pat of butter. Wasting no time, Libra dipped her spoon into the thick broth. While she ate, Voca, who had busied herself all day absorbing the information available through Earth's electronic media, presented Libra with a synopsis of her most immediately useful findings.

Meanwhile, Hank, who had followed closely behind Libra and had seen her enter the little pile of redwood boughs, saw a light emanating from within the branches. He also smelled something heavenly. Creeping stealthily, he came as close as he dared and peeped in. Libra had carelessly left the door open, and Hank could see her spooning succulent morsels of seafood into her mouth. Though he had recently eaten, he found the aroma irresistible, and he crept closer and closer to the edge of the mound. At last, torn between his appetite on the one hand, and his mounting trepidation on the other, he reluctantly turned around and started back down the mountain. In his mind, however, a simple plan was unfolding. He would return to this spot again, soon, when Libra was away.

Chapter 8
Hank's Discovery

SHORTLY AFTER LIBRA BOARDED THE BUS, Hank decided to have an adventure of his own. He was haunted by the previous night's vision of Libra sitting in the glow of what looked like a cozy cave underneath the pile of redwood boughs. And so, following a short after-breakfast nap on the picnic table, he roused himself to investigate. With a flick of his fluffy tail he scrambled over the fence and set off up the mountain in search of the strange cat's secret hiding place.

He was soon in sight of the meadow where Voca had landed, and he had no trouble spotting the mound of redwood boughs that he had seen the night before. He felt his heart pound and his fur stand on end. Stealthily he approached, stalking in slow motion, stretching out his back paws to their maximum length as he reached forward with his front paws, then slowly bringing the back paws forward for the next step, threading them carefully through the weeds so as not to disturb a single blade of grass. All his muscles were taut, ready to launch him down the mountain at the first sign of danger, and his feline senses were on full alert. But all was perfectly calm. Not a sound issued from the mound, and the meadow was alive with the carefree, cheerful buzzing of insects and the chirping and singing of birds. And as he crept forward the sun beat down on his thick fur, making him feel uncomfortably warm.

Closer and closer he approached, until he arrived at the opening in the mound through which he had spied Libra the previous night. A small metallic ramp led to an open door, and Hank stepped onto it gingerly. Finally, growing impatient with all this stealth, which didn't seem to be really necessary, he threw caution to the winds and strode boldly into the ship. Once inside, he was amazed to see a room full of blinking lights, panels with switches, a large television screen, and a variety of small shelves and compartments all of gleaming metal. He was so mesmerized that he didn't notice the door closing behind him.

"Good morning, Hank." said Voca.

Hank started and turned to run out, but the door had disappeared. In a panic he dashed round and round the cabin searching for an exit.

"Don't be frightened, Hank," said Voca reassuringly.

But Hank was anything but reassured, and he began to mew piteously.

Voca recorded his mewing and checked it against her database of ancient Gatosian languages.

"Aha!" she exclaimed at last. "His language is remarkably similar to the most ancient of all Gatosian tongues, Meow, which was reconstructed from scratchings found on the walls of caves. I'll try it out on him."

"Meeoww, brrow brrrrroww," she said, which when spoken using the proper tonal inflection means, "There's nothing to be frightened of."

"Meee-ew, meee-ew, brrrrrrow?" ("Why shouldn't I be frightened?") answered Hank, shocked to hear words he could understood.

"Eee-ew, brrrrrr meee-ew brrowww," said Voca. ("Because I'm your friend.")

"Mew-meow   brr-eee-ow?"
("How can I be sure?") answered
Hank.

The words were barely out
of his mouth when a compart-
ment in the kitchen console
opened, and a plate of the most
heavenly slices of broiled salmon
filet that Hank had ever
smelled was set before
him by a mechanical
arm, which then
retracted into the
wall. His fears forgot-
ten, Hank bent over the
plate and polished off
Voca's offering in no time. After sniffing around the plate
for stray scraps, he sat up and washed his face with his
forepaws and licked the fur around his neck, switching his
tail back and forth with satisfaction. Then he waited
expectantly. Perhaps the invisible friendly cat who spoke
to him from behind the walls would soon show herself. He
looked to his right and to his left, but no cat emerged. No
matter, he thought to himself, and lay down on his side to
wait comfortably.

Seeing that he was no longer frightened, but that he
was confused about her whereabouts, Voca projected an
image of herself on the monitor as a short-haired, green-
eyed calico. Without moving from his side on the polished
metal floor, Hank lifted his gaze to the calico cat on the
screen above the console. Although still confused, he was
glad to have someone or something to look at. Then Voca,
in the guise of the green-eyed calico, again began speaking
to Hank in Meow. She spoke slowly and softly to avoid
startling him and to gain his confidence. In the simplest
possible terms, Voca explained to Hank that she and Libra

had come from another world, Gatos, so far away from planet Earth that it was impossible even to imagine, and that they were on a scientific mission to explore new solar systems. Hank was amazed to discover that he could understand what Voca was saying, even though what she was saying was totally outside his experience as an Earthling cat. He was astounded to hear that the rulers of Gatos were cats much like himself, except more technologically advanced. He sat up on his haunches and began to purr with pride. She explained how she had caught hundreds of computer viruses while downloading the Internet, and that they would have crashed in the Pacific Ocean if the Commander hadn't saved the day. Then she had sneezed, damaging one of her essential components, and now they were marooned on Earth, unable to return to Gatos. Finally, she told him that the Commander had embarked on a mission to enlist the aid of a computer company to help them build a new nanochip. It was especially dangerous because humans were so unpredictable and didn't regard cats as their equals.

When Voca finished her tale, a look of concern came over Hank's normally placid face.

"Meee-ew, brrroow-mew mrrrw?" ("How can I help?") he asked.

"First, you must learn modern Gatosian," she said. "It will be difficult, but you'll need it to communicate with Commander Shimagrimicka, who hasn't the time to learn Meow. Gatosian will allow you to express yourself more precisely, which may come in handy later on. We'll begin our first lesson immediately, so please concentrate. . ."

Poor Hank! It was all so totally alien to him. No one had ever spoken to him like this or given him so much new information all at once—not even his mother. His head was spinning. Perhaps it was all a dream. He dug the claws of his left paw into his right paw until it hurt, but he didn't wake up. Then Voca began pronouncing Gatosian words and giving him their equivalents in Meow. She insisted that he repeat after her. Often there was no Meow equivalent, and then she showed him a picture on the television screen. Never had he had to think so hard for such a long time. Finally, when he felt he was too exhausted to think even one more thought, the cabin door slid open.

"Very good, Hank," said Voca in Meow. "Return here tomorrow for lunch and for your second lesson."

Hank got up and walked slowly down the ramp. Before alighting on the ground, he turned back toward the open door.

"Good-bye, Voca," he said in perfect Gatosian.

"Good-bye, Hank. See you tomorrow," she replied. Voca's door slid shut and Hank turned to leave. It was late afternoon, and the sun cast long, cool shadows on the ground. Imagine! A planet where cats were in charge! Commander Libra Shimagrimicka was a distinguished emissary from a planet ruled by cats, and she was in trouble. He resolved to do everything in his power to help, no matter how difficult the task. His chest swelled with a new pride as he strode down the mountain path. He could hardly wait to report his discovery to his sister, Pinny. Pinny was very clever, and he knew she'd want to help, too.

"*Competition,* Jug," Rolf Trammel corrected. "Let's stick to the high road."

"Yeah, dat's what I meant," said Jug Maraud. ". . . Rubbing out da competition, meaning Cameron Computers. If I could have the lights off and the foist slide . . ."

Maraud pulled a screen down over the Dogma logo on the rear wall while one of the men in the white suits switched off the lights and drew the curtains. The room was plunged into darkness. A moment later the slide projector, which was on a stand at the far end of the room opposite the screen, was turned on, and a large rectangle of light, flecked with motes of dust and assorted hairs, appeared behind Mr. Trammel. While Jug Maraud fumbled with the remote, Libra, emboldened by the sudden darkness, lifted up the tablecloth and draped it over her head to get a better view.

The first slide showed a red brick building that might have been a converted warehouse. The slide was of very poor quality, and the ancient projector made a dreadful racket.

Staring at the screen, Libra suddenly realized that she hadn't eaten since breakfast and that she was sitting beneath the refreshment table. Now that the room was darkened and all eyes were focused on the screen, she decided it would be perfectly safe for her to quickly steal a snack and return to her hiding place. Emerging from under the tablecloth, she hopped silently onto the tabletop and stood for a moment surveying what was left of the food. Carefully picking up a plate and fork, she helped herself to half a roast beef sandwich, a slice of apple pie, and a glass of punch. These she placed near the front edge of the table before dropping noiselessly back down to the floor. Retrieving her plate and glass from the edge of the table, she returned to her hiding place to watch the show.

"Dis is da Cameron Computer Company," Mr. Maraud intoned, ". . . founded by da couple, Felix and

Adele Cameron. I tink dere both retired professors or somethin'. . . ."

The next slide was a photograph taken from a newspaper article showing a middle-aged couple in formal attire.

"Dis slide shows da Camerons gettin' an onerous degree from some college in England for some speriments dey did on *superitivity*—or somethin' like dat. Whatever it was, it was s'posed to make computers run faster. Big deal!"

"So," mused Libra while munching her roast beef sandwich, "sounds like the Camerons were trying to introduce superconductivity into microchips. A promising beginning. This is the company I should be dealing with. . . ."

Jug Maraud continued. "Da point is that if somethin' ain't done about Cameron Computers and der superitivity, it could cause problems for us here at Dogma."

Sobered by Mr. Maraud's words, the Dogma board members exchanged worried glances.

"But da news ain't all bad," continued Jug Maraud, wearing a sly smile. "About five months ago, I'm sorry ta hafta report, Dr. Cameron was killed in a car accident."

Mr. Trammel clucked his tongue and shook his head somberly. "Tragic," he said, with a malevolent grin.

"Yes, very tragic," agreed Jug Maraud, behind a barely concealed smirk. "It seems he was driving back from da univoisity on Highway 17 on a rainy night, and lost control of his car. We all know what a dangerous stretch of road dat is. His car skidded off the highway, rolled down an embankment, hit a large rock at the bottom of a ravine and exploded. Da poor man died instantly. Da police ruled it was an accident."

"What about the insurance company, Jug?" asked the representative from Berlin. "We heard there was a potential problem there."

"Oh yeah, one of dem claims investigators, Carlos Valdez, tried to make a case for 'suspicious circumstances,' but dere wasn't no evidence. The explosion blew it all to smithereens." Maraud smiled.

At this point a large gentleman wearing a black tee shirt, dark sunglasses, and a red gang bandanna over his bald head, snickered so loudly that heads turned in his direction.

"I fear I've stumbled on something truly evil," Libra reflected.

Mr. Trammel stood up.

"If I may, Jug, and for the record, I'd like to say a few words about this unfortunate incident. We at Dogma were all shocked and greatly saddened by the news and sent our condolences to his family. Even though Dr. Cameron was one of Dogma's fiercest competitors, we bore him no ill will. In fact, I attended the funeral and made a donation of several Dogma computers to the local high school in Dr. Cameron's name."

Nods of approval greeted the revelation of Mr. Trammel's touching act of generosity.

Jug Maraud continued. "Mr. Trammel also made several offers ta buy da company, but so far Adele Cameron has refused. She was almost ready ta accept, but den her daughter, Cathy, persuaded her not to."

Libra's eyes opened wide in amazement as a new slide appeared on the screen. It was Cathy! Hank's human! What a fool she'd been! She should have recognized the name Cameron immediately. The solution to her problem had been practically in her own back yard!

"So dat's how t'ings stand, Ladies and Gentlemen," Jug Maraud continued. "Our aim is ta convince dis Cathy Cameron and her mother, Adele, dat it's in everyone's best interest for dem ta accept Mr. Trammel's kind offer. Udderwise dey could get hoit."

With a sudden flourish, Jug Maraud thumped his fist

upon his chest and swung dramatically down onto his stool. The violent gesture startled Mr. Kluliss and made him spill his coffee. Surprised by the dual sensations of warmth and wetness on his thigh as coffee spilled from the table onto his trousers, Rolf Trammel mis-swallowed a piece of Danish and fell into a fit of coughing, while those around the table averted their gaze, pretending not to notice. However, it soon became apparent from his bulging eyes and the bluish cast of his skin that Mr. Trammel was running out of oxygen, and Mr. Kluliss frantically set about thumping him on the back, while Mr. Trammel angrily fended him off. Finally the errant morsel dislodged from Mr. Trammel's windpipe, and he soon recovered his breath and his dignity.

"Yes, thank you, Jug," he said, still clearing his throat. "After the meeting I wonder if you and Mr. Carne would be so kind as to meet privately with me in my office to discuss what . . . steps . . . should be taken."

Libra, who had been listening intently, grasped the significance of Mr. Trammel's words immediately, and a shiver ran down her back as she thought of the danger to Cathy and her mother.

on their skateboards. Grumbling and swearing, Rolf Trammel called off the chase.

"The cat got away," he said, "but we have this!" He held up Libra's communicator clenched in his fist, with the gold chain dangling down. As he squeezed it angrily, the communicator suddenly emitted a crackling noise, and a high-pitched voice could be heard. It sounded like mewing.

Then it was silent.

"What was that?" asked Secretary Kluliss.

"Sounded like a cat," replied Ms. Daggett.

"Don't be ridiculous. Cats can't talk!" snapped Ms. Debbitz.

Rolf Trammel smiled. "Jug, take this over to the telecommunications department and track down whoever is sending the signal. No one spies on Dogma and gets away with it. No one, do you hear? I'm authorizing you to unleash the Marauders!"

Chapter 14
Invasion of the Marauders

A FTER BREAKFAST HANK AND PINNY SAT a few meters apart on the tile patio and washed their faces and ears. Hank, who was less thorough than Pinny, finished first and watched his sister through half-opened eyes, occasionally licking his thick fluffy coat. He wanted to tell Pinny about his encounters with Libra and Voca, but he wasn't sure Voca would approve, since their mission was top secret. Pinny finished her grooming and started toward the fence at the side of the house. Hank knew that after jumping onto the fence, she would climb onto the large loquat tree, and from an overhanging branch drop down onto the roof, where she would spend the better part of the morning studying bird behavior. Pinny's study had begun with shooing away starlings from the roof, preventing them from nesting among the clay tiles—for which she had been rewarded by Adele with copious praise, pets, and occasional treats. However, Pinny was fascinated by flight, and soon took an interest in the lives of the feathered creatures. At last she had secretly allowed a family of bluebirds to nest in the corner of the roof where Adele wouldn't see them. Recently several eggs had hatched, and Pinny had been observing the efforts of the two parents to feed their three demanding chicks. She was particularly looking forward to observing their first flying lessons. Now, as Pinny approached the fence on her way to the roof, Hank made a quick decision.

"I know something you don't know," he said proudly (speaking in Meow, of course).

"What?" replied Pinny.

"I know a cat even smarter than you," said Hank.

Pinny looked at him doubtfully.

"Who?"

"The one who visited us the other day. Her name is *Libra*! She's the commander of a spaceship from the planet Gatos, and her ship's name is Voca," Hank replied. But since many of his words were Gatosian, Pinny had no idea what he was saying. It sounded like gibberish.

"What are you saying, Hank? I can't understand you!"

"I'm learning *Gatosian*," said Hank proudly. "Come with me, Pinny, and I'll show you. You can meet Voca."

Pinny was very skeptical, to say the least. She was afraid her poor brother had been sniffing too much catnip. Hank ran up to the back fence and scrambled to the top.

"Come on, Pinny!" he called out from the top of the fence. "You won't be sorry."

"Oh, all right," said Pinny, "but this had better be good. I think the chicks are going to take their first flying lessons today."

Hank dropped down to the other side of the fence. Pinny followed close behind, and together they started up the trail leading to the meadow where Voca lay hidden.

When they arrived at the mound of redwood boughs, Hank led Pinny through the branches, up the short ramp and into the cabin of the ship. Pinny was impressed.

"Voca, I brought my sister Pinny with me today," Hank exclaimed.

Voca immediately displayed her calico cat image on the monitor so that Hank and Pinny would be able to

relate to it.

"You didn't tell me you had a sister, Hank! I'm pleased to meet you, Pinny," said Voca in Meow.

"I'm glad to meet you, too, Voca," Pinny replied, gazing up at the calico cat.

"Where's Libra? Has she come back yet?" Hank asked in Gatosian.

"The last time I heard from the Commander she was on her way to the Dogma Computer Company, and I haven't heard from her since. About an hour ago I received a signal from her communicator. At first I thought it was the Commander, but when I responded there was no answer." Her voice trembled slightly. "I'm terribly worried something may have happened to her. What if she's been captured? What then? Oh my! I *warned* her not to get mixed up with Dogma! I've been researching that company on the Internet, and I can tell you, its board of directors reads like the FBI's most wanted list!"

Although he understood only a fraction of what Voca had said, her anxiety was contagious, and Hank's confidence was shaken.

"I hope Commander Shimagrimicka's all right," he said softly.

Pinny nudged her brother. Knowing no Gatosian, she felt left out of the conversation, and from Hank's worried tone of voice it sounded as though there was trouble.

"My sister, Pinny, would like to learn Gatosian," said Hank. "Would you teach her, Voca?"

"Why, yes, of course, Hank!" replied Voca. "How rude of me to forget! Pinny," she mewed warmly in Meow. "Please forgive my bad manners. We'll begin your Gatosian lessons immediately."

And for the rest of the day Voca gave Pinny and Hank Gatosian lessons, regaling them with stories of Gatosian history and of the illustrious career of Commander Shimagrimicka. Pinny, who was very quick, learned easily, and by the end of the day she was speaking passable Gatosian—better, in fact, than Hank's. Voca told her she showed great promise, and Pinny beamed with pride.

"Voca says I'm very smart," said Pinny proudly, as they headed back down the trail at the end of the day. "Of course, not as smart as Commander Shimagricka," she added, "but then she's from the planet Gatos, where *everyone* is smart. She also studied at the Space Academy. I wonder if I could ever be a space cadet like Commander Shimagrimicka? . . ."

But Hank was much too preoccupied worrying about Libra's safety to answer. Several times during the day their lessons had been interrupted when Voca had received strange, incomprehensible signals from Libra's communicator, but after a few attempts, she stopped responding for fear the communicator had fallen into the wrong hands. They had also heard the sound of helicopters flying low overhead, causing Voca to shut down most of her systems in alarm. Hank and Pinny peeked outside and saw the helicopter making long sweeping runs across the sky as though searching for something.

The second day passed by much like the first. Voca was even more upset because she had still not heard from Libra, and there were more alarming signals from the communicator and the sound of helicopters overhead. Still, Voca went on with their lessons. Besides becoming fluent in Gatosian, Pinny was also making progress in Gatosian mathematics, although Hank preferred Gatosian poetry, particularly the descriptions of the ocean at night illuminated by three moons, which seemed very strange and wonderful to him. Voca had also yielded to Pinny's repeated requests to teach her basic aviation skills, which pleased the little tabby cat no end. Using the large monitor above the console as a flight simulator, Voca allowed Pinny to maneuver an imaginary spacecraft manually from take-off to landing. Pinny was so excited that she kept scratching the keyboard instead of simply pushing the buttons.

"Pinny, please keep your claws retracted!" Voca pleaded. "They only get in the way. Now I see where you get your name. You're trying to make a pincushion out of my console!"

"I'm very sorry, Voca," smiled Pinny guiltily. But she was much too gleeful about learning to fly to be totally contrite.

While Pinny was practicing her take-offs and landings, Hank kept peering nervously out the door. The helicopters had disappeared, and for the first time in days the meadow had become peaceful again. The birds resumed their singing, and he could even hear the breezes stirring the tall dry grass.

But slowly, imperceptibly at first, he became aware of an alien presence approaching the meadow, a low muttering noise that grew louder and louder by degrees, until it became an ugly, fearsome, menacing roar.

"What's that sound?" asked Pinny nervously.

"I don't know, but I'm going outside to investigate. You stay here and guard Voca," he added.

"Be careful, Hank," said Voca.

Hank crouched low and crept down the ramp. As soon as his paws touched the ground he scurried over to the path. As he looked toward the horizon he saw something that made his fur stand on end, for heading towards him, both on and off the path, was a plague of large black motorcycles, resembling giant locusts with wheels. They were stirring up a dust storm as they came, and Hank could see that the riders were as loathsome-looking as their vehicles. Huge, pierced and tattooed from head to foot, wearing gang bandannas, dirty T-shirts and worn-out black leather jackets, they were bearing down on Voca's hiding place with alarming speed. Even at this distance, Hank could see that their faces were twisted with malevolence, the ugliness of their mood apparently fueled by whatever they had drunk from the bottles that they tossed onto the meadow.

Terrified, Hank's first impulse was to run down the trail in the opposite direction, down the mountainside and over the fence to his own safe back yard. But then he thought of Voca, and Libra's mission, and the planet Gatos, where cats were the rulers of an advanced civilization, and he knew that he could not run away.

He guessed that the motorcyclists were, in fact, looking for Voca. Why else had the helicopters been buzzing overhead for the last two days, if not to track Voca's whereabouts? In a matter of seconds they would be spread out in front of her hiding place. Looking back over his shoulder he could see, glinting in the sunlight, a corner of the spacecraft's ramp extending from the redwood pile, and it seemed inevitable that one of the gang would spot it. He had to do something, but what?

Arching over the narrow dirt trail was the huge, lichen-encrusted branch of a venerable old live oak tree. Gazing upward into its foliage, Hank had an idea. Nimbly he climbed up the thick trunk and crept along the middle of the wide branch until he was directly over the path. There he flattened himself, so that he was virtually invisible against the gray bark, among the dark green leaves and gauzy, hanging lichens.

He was barely in place when the motorcycle gang arrived, and, at a signal from their leader who had stopped on the path directly below him, they pulled up just opposite Voca's hiding place, gunning their motors.

"This is the spot where the choppers traced the signal," said Frank Carne, peering down at a map.

"I don't see nuttin'," said a blond-haired woman with a large scar across her right cheek. "Just a bunch of grass and trees and stuff."

"You *sure* you know how to read maps?" someone yelled from the back row, eliciting chuckles and guffaws from the other gang members.

Frank Carne glared darkly back at his unruly cohorts.

"I don't see nuthin' either, but just in case, let's torch the place!" he snarled. Pulling a wad of newspapers from his saddlebag, he lit it with a cigarette lighter and threw it down into the weeds beside the trail. The dry grass ignited instantly and crackled into flame.

"Now fan out and burn down this whole meadow," Frank Carne ordered. "We'll smoke 'em out!"

Suddenly he screamed.

All eyes turned to Carne, and to their astonishment, they saw a large gray and white tomcat atop their leader's head, furiously raking his claws over the tender flesh of Carne's bare scalp.

"That must be the cat Mr. Trammel told us about!" cried the blond-haired woman.

"No, Jug said the cat was all black. This one's gray and white," observed a burly brute wearing dark glasses with a bandanna tied over his pony tail.

"Yeah, but it was pretty dark in the conference room," replied the blond. "Maybe it only *looked* black."

"Aaaaiiiieeeeeeeee!" screamed Frank Carne. "I don't care what color it is! Get it off me!"

Hank bounded off Carne's head and scurried out across the meadow through the thick grasses towards the woods.

"Catch that cat!" shouted Frank Carne.

Violently gunning their engines, the Marauders motorcycle gang lurched forward across the meadow, tearing up the vegetation and spewing dark exhaust into the pure mountain air. Hank could hear the sound of the tires smashing down the tall grasses behind him as he ran, darting this way and that to throw them off his trail. They were gaining on him inch by inch, and he was beginning to run out of breath. In another moment they would be upon him. But the woods were just ahead. He plunged into the very densest section, thick with trees and rocks and with poison oak carpeting the forest floor and hanging like lianas from the branches. Hank scampered through the thick greenery without difficulty. But the Marauders were stymied. In vain they tried to force their motorcycles through the tangled, rocky undergrowth, but they repeatedly tipped over and rolled onto the forest floor.

"Hey, isn't this stuff poison oak we're wallowing in?" someone asked at last.

"Oh, yeah, you're right, it is!"

"Let's get out of here! I'm real allergic to poison oak. I need some calamine lotion soon or I'm gonna be hospitalized!" cried the blond-haired woman.

"Wait a minute! What about the cat?" cried Mr. Carne.

"Forget it!" said the man with the bandanna. "It's just a cat! Let's go home and shower! Anybody got some brown soap?"

Muttering and grumbling to themselves, the Marauders pushed their motorcycles out of the woods and back onto the meadow.

"Wimps!" shouted Mr. Carne, stamping his feet in the poison oak, but to no avail, for the roar of the engines drowned out his words as his colleagues sped away. Eventually, even Mr. Carne admitted defeat, and dejectedly followed the other gang members, tenderly caressing the bleeding hatchwork of deep scratches engraved in his scalp.

Although the Marauders had suffered a humiliating defeat at the paws of Hank, the fire that started when Frank Carne tossed the burning wad of newspaper into the grass was spreading rapidly and increasing in intensity. Pinny, who had witnessed Hank's heroic action, saw with alarm that the fire was heading in the direction of the little pile of branches under which they were hiding and would soon engulf them in flames. Even if Voca's insulation would protect her from the heat, the redwood boughs covering her would be burned away and she would be exposed to overflying aircraft. Already the acrid smoke was filling the interior of the cabin, and Voca's fire alarms were buzzing. If only Commander Shimagrimicka would return!

"Voca! The fire's coming at us! What are we going to do?" she cried.

"Look underneath the console, Pinny! Do you see a fire extinguisher?"

Pinny peered under the console. She saw a small, red canister with a nozzle and a white button on top.

"I see it!" said Pinny.

"Carry it outside, point the nozzle at the flames, and push the white button."

"I can't!" Pinny cried.

"Yes you can, Pinny. You can do it!" Voca's voice was calm but firm.

"No I can't, Voca!" Pinny replied, her voice quavering. "I'm just an ordinary Earthling cat. I'm not like Commander Shimagrimicka. I can't even pick things up the way she can!"

"You can do it in your own way," Voca assured her. "I know you can. I have confidence in you!"

"I'll try!" said Pinny, almost in tears. Reaching with her right paw, she rolled the red canister out to the center of the cabin. Then, sliding her front paws under it, she cradled it in her arms and carried it down the ramp and out onto the meadow, walking on her back paws in an unfamiliar gait. Turning her head to right and left, she quickly identified the burning edge of the fire, and managed to drag the red canister over to it. Mounting it vertically on the ground, she pointed the nozzle at the flames and pushed the white button.

"Whhhhishhhhhhhh!"

A gust of cool powdery foam shot out of the nozzle, coating the ground a frosty white and instantly dousing the fire.

"That was fun!" said Pinny, no longer feeling like a helpless Earthling cat. Wrapping her paws around the nozzle, she dragged the canister over to another part of the blaze and pushed the white button again.

"Wwwhhisshhhhhhhh!" went the canister and the white foam quickly extinguished the flames.

"I can do it!" Pinny shouted, as she rolled the canister to the last remaining section of the fire.

"Whhhisshhhhhh! Whhhishhhhhh! Whhissshhhhh!"

And in no time, Pinny had put the fire out. Drawing her right paw across her brow, she looked up in time to see her brother, Hank, approaching. He looked a little bedraggled, and his coat was covered with cobwebs, sticks and leaves, but he was smiling.

"Hi, Pinny! Nice job! I'm proud of you!"

"I didn't think I could do it, Hank, but Voca believed in me. She said I could. But what about you? I saw the motorcyclists chase you across the meadow. Are you all right?"

"I'm fine," replied Hank, "but I think those motorcyclists are in for a few sleepless nights after rolling around in the poison oak. I was well-hidden in an old foxhole while they were thrashing." Hank looked out across the meadow. "You know, Pinny," he reflected, "ever since we learned Gatosian, I feel we can do all sorts of things we couldn't do before."

"It's all in having it explained properly," returned Pinny. "Once you understand how it's done, it's easy!"

Brother and sister stood in silence for a moment. The afternoon had given way to evening, and the western sky was aglow with purples and oranges. Already the symphony of crickets and frogs was beginning, and the air was turning cooler.

"Do you think they'll come back, Hank?" asked Pinny.

"The motorcyclists? I'm afraid so, since they didn't achieve their objective."

"If only the Commander were here!" Pinny exclaimed. "She'd know what to do!"

"Let's see how Voca's doing," said Hank, and they returned to the spacecraft.

Chapter 16
Schrödinger's Fish and the Green Medallion

THE DRIVE BACK WITH LIBRA marked a turning point in Cathy's life. Once she had recovered from the shock of being spoken to by a cat, whom she now recognized as the same statuesque black cat who had wandered through her house only a few days before, she could begin to comprehend what Libra was actually saying to her. Seated with her legs crossed and her right paw resting jauntily on the door handle, Libra was the image of sophistication as she patiently recounted her scientific mission, how she had traveled in space-time for one hundred years through the vast regions of the Milky Way Galaxy in the stasis chamber, nearly crash-landing in the Pacific Ocean before touching down in a meadow in the Santa Cruz Mountains near Los Gatos. She went on to describe her chance meeting with Hank, how Voca had caught a cold from some computer viruses while downloading the Internet, how Voca's sneeze had damaged her furry logic superconducting anti-matter power-interface nanochip, and how Libra had ventured forth to find a computer company to help construct a new one. This quest had brought her to the Dogma Computer Company.

"Why didn't you tell me all this when you first came to the house?" Cathy complained. "To think, I treated you like an ordinary cat! We could have helped you. My mother is a computer engineer, and we even own a computer company."

"I know that now," said Libra. "But I had no way of knowing it then. Also, I had assumed that cats would be in charge here. I guess I was a little suspicious of humans at first. At any rate, my instructions were to minimize contact with Earthlings. That's why I decided to go straight to the top, to the president of a computer company."

Cathy was aghast as Libra went on to describe how she had been delivered to the Dogma loading dock in a cardboard box, how she had narrowly escaped being crushed under the weight of a tower of broken equipment, her encounter with the pit bulls in the elevator, how she had infiltrated the Dogma international board of directors meeting by hiding under the refreshment table, her daring escape and fall from the sixth floor window, her harassment by Mama Palm Rat and her precipitous descent to the ground, which had led, finally, to her being rescued by some passing school children.

"You could have been killed!" exclaimed Cathy. "Dogma's a rough crowd, and they play hardball."

Libra nodded knowingly, although she had no idea what "hardball" was. She then began to relate what she had heard at the meeting from her hiding place under the refreshment table. Cathy was greatly amused as Libra mimicked Rolf Trammel's purse-lipped address to his assembled CEOs, his obsession with profit margins, his worship of mediocrity, and his dread of new ideas.

After they had both enjoyed a good laugh at Rolf Trammel's expense, they fell silent, and all was quiet in the car except for the hum of the engine and the sound of tires hissing and lapping over the asphalt. Since it was difficult for Libra to see out of the window while sitting, she stood up on the seat to get a better view, leaning forward with her front paws on the dashboard. As they pulled up along side a burgundy-colored Lexus in the right lane, Libra gazed at the driver—an elderly woman with stylishly cut snow-white hair. Beside her, stretched out on the top of the seat, was a Siamese cat with haughty blue eyes. The Siamese glanced down at Libra with a superior air. Libra smiled and waved, and the Siamese nearly fell from her perch.

"The whole thing would be even funnier," said Cathy at length, "if Dogma didn't have a stranglehold on the industry. But Trammel and his cronies have driven all of the other smaller companies out of business. Once he's acquired a company he usually shuts it down or moves it outside the country, throwing hundreds of people out of work. Now he's trying to take over Cameron Computers. Hardly a day goes by that he doesn't call my mother and hound her to sell out. I'm afraid that she's going to give in to him one of these days. Ever since my father died, things have been going wrong at the company. Shipments have been lost. Retailers have cancelled their orders. We're losing money hand over fist and our creditors are losing their patience. I'm convinced Trammel's behind all this, but I can't prove it. It's ironic because just before my father died he telephoned my mother about the results of an experiment he'd been working on at U. C. Santa Cruz. He said the data was just coming in and that it looked very promising. Something totally unexpected had turned up, something neither of them had anticipated, which caused a big boost in superconductivity at room temperatures. Some kind of contaminant in the ceramic matrix. He wouldn't talk about it over the phone, but he said he would bring the data home with him. He was on his way home with his notebook when he was killed in an accident. . . ."

Cathy swallowed hard and fought back the tears. They had arrived at the Los Gatos exit and she pulled off the freeway and headed north on Redwood Drive. Libra was remembering the early Gatosian experiments on superconductivity during the last century, and she could guess what the contaminant might have been—prrrftiium, most likely, or maybe screechium, one of the first anti-matter elements discovered. She would have loved to tell Cathy all she knew, which would have catapulted Earthling computer science into a brilliant new future, but, alas, it was forbidden, and so she bit her tongue. Besides, she had a feeling that Cathy would one day solve the problem on her own. Why deprive her of the joy of the discovery?

"What happened to your father's notebook?" asked Libra as they stood waiting for a stoplight.

"The police never found it," answered Cathy. "We never found out what happened to it. Maybe it was destroyed in the fire."

"What do you think really happened?" Libra inquired gently after a pause. The light went green and Cathy pulled out.

"Think? I don't know what to think. The police insisted that it was an accident. But the insurance investigator, Carlos Valdez, told my mother that he wasn't so sure. He hinted that my father's . . . death . . ." (she still had difficulty saying the word) "might not have been an accident. He said we should be careful. . . ." Her voice trailed off.

Libra looked out the window and watched the passing scene: service stations, restaurants, shops, houses on tree-lined avenues, and people. Only people. Cats were invisible here on Earth—unlike Gatos, where every place you looked you saw cats of every color, shade, and stripe, quietly going about their business or just having fun. Not in living memory, at least, had a cat been murdered on Gatos. Scratched, yes. Bitten, yes. But not murdered.

Cathy turned down a side street and Libra recognized the corner where she had caught the bus. A few blocks later they pulled into the driveway of Cathy's house. Adele's car, like Cathy's fuel-cell car only dark blue, was already parked in front of the garage. Libra was deep in thought. She was considering how to reveal her own suspicions about Dr. Cameron's death without upsetting the young woman too much.

"It looks like my mother's home," said Cathy. "I hope she's not mad at me. We haven't been getting along so well lately. Meeting you is going to come as quite a surprise." She opened the car door and was about to get out when Libra suddenly reached out her left paw and touched Cathy's arm.

"Cathy," Libra said somberly, "I heard other things at that meeting at Dogma that tend to confirm Carlos Valdez's suspicions."

Cathy turned swiftly to face her.

"What do you mean?" she asked.

"Have you heard of Jug Maraud?" asked Libra.

"According to the grapevine, he's part of the Las Vegas gambling scene. Worked for one of the big casinos as a bouncer. Do you know what a bouncer is?"

Libra nodded. Although she'd never heard of a "bouncer" before, she could easily imagine what one did. What intrigued Libra the most, however, was that Cathy had learned the information from a grapevine. "Apparently some Earthling plants have evolved speech," she reflected, and made a mental note to report this remarkable fact to the Gatosian Botanical Society.

"Anyway," Cathy continued, "it's rumored that Maraud's connected with the mob. You know, the Mafia? A few years ago he was indicted for fraud and racketeering, but a famous lawyer got him off. What's Maraud got to do with my father?"

Cathy's description of Maraud was consistent with Libra's worst fears. During her first day in Los Gatos she had watched TV shows on Voca's terminal that showed what the Mafia was all about. It seemed more and more likely that Dr. Cameron had indeed been the victim of foul play. The question was, what could be done about the imminent danger to Cathy and her mother? Of course she would have to warn them, despite her instructions to refrain from interfering in Earthling affairs.

"Let's go inside," she said," and I'll tell you everything I know. Then I've got to get back to Voca, who's probably stuck in an infinite series of iterative worrying."

Cathy smiled, and the two of them walked hand in paw up to the doorstep.

Needless to say, Adele Cameron's extensive scientific background in no way prepared her for her introduction to Libra. But once she had gotten past her initial incredulity, like Cathy, she warmed up to the small but distinguished visitor from across the galaxy, especially when it became clear that Libra's knowledge of physics and computer science far exceeded her own—or anyone else's on Earth for that matter. She was also glad to have a civil conversation with her daughter for the first time in many days. She listened intently while Cathy repeated the story of Libra's adventures thus far, frowning at the mention of Dogma computers and Rolf Trammel. Turning to Libra, she immediately offered to help her construct a new anti-matter nanochip, although she advised Libra that no one on Earth had yet succeeded in producing an anti-matter element.

"As president of Cameron Computers," she declared, "I put my company at your disposal. Even if Dogma Computers were to offer to help you make a new nanochip, I'd advise against accepting their offer, since the final product probably wouldn't work anyway, if their computers are any indication."

As it was already around 5:30 PM, they decided to put off their more weighty discussions until after supper. Libra, who was too proud to confess how hungry she was,

was glad that the subject had come up naturally. Cathy got out the large wooden cutting board and two sharp knives (handing her guest the smaller one), and she and Libra—standing on a high stool—sliced cucumbers, tomatoes, lettuce, bell peppers, and avocados for a salad, while Adele heated up a pot of hearty clam chowder. It reminded Libra of summer vacations by the seashore at beautiful Green Eye Bay near North Pawtuckett where, as a kitten, she used to help her mother prepare the evening meal.

"That's funny," said Adele as she stirred the chowder. "I haven't seen either Hank or Pinny all day, and it's nearly dinner time."

"I don't know where they are." said Cathy. "I was looking for them earlier, but I couldn't find them."

Libra cleared her throat.

"I think I can probably explain," she said while trimming off the leaves and roots of a plump red radish with her paring knife. "Voca has been giving Hank lessons in Gatosian. He may have brought Pinny along, too. They're probably both up in the meadow right now, and if I know Voca, they're probably both fluent in Gatosian by now."

With a series of lightning quick strokes, Libra cleaved her trimmed radish into a heap of paper-thin disks, which she then scooped onto her knife blade and—in one smooth motion—tossed into the salad bowl.

Cathy and Adele were delighted with Libra's culinary skills. They were also astonished to hear that their own two cats, whom they had hitherto thought of only as dumb animals, were capable of interacting with a computer and of learning a highly sophisticated foreign language.

"This certainly does change my attitude toward them," said Adele Cameron.

"Yes," agreed Cathy. "I won't know how to address Hank and Pinny when I see them next. Usually I just pick them up and pet them and talk to them in—like—baby talk! Now I'd be totally embarrassed to do that. . . ."

Libra could see that Cathy found this new wrinkle in her relationship with Hank and Pinny somewhat disconcerting.

"I wouldn't worry about that," she said reassuringly. "Hank and Pinny are still Earthling cats. They've grown up as Earthlings and they're used to Earthling customs. They'd only feel bad if you stopped being affectionate and petting them. But you can still show them respect in other ways."

"I guess we'll just have to adjust our thinking a little," said Cathy.

"Yes, we certainly will, dear," replied her mother. "About a lot of things! How's the salad coming?"

"It's done," said Cathy.

"Good. Let's have chowder first. Perhaps we can persuade our honored guest to tell us a little bit more about her marvelous planet and, especially, about the state of Gatosian science, at least as much as she's permitted to tell us."

Thus encouraged, Libra, who always enjoyed the limelight, held forth for the next hour and a half about her favorite subject—Gatos. Between sips, bites, and nibbles, she fondly recalled the geography, geology, natural history and feline history of Gatos. Adele and Cathy showered her with so many questions that she barely had time to answer one when another was posed.

"One thing I've been wondering about," began Cathy. "You said that the journey from Gatos took 100 years, yet according to our astronomers, the nearest habitable planet outside our solar system is 100,000 light years away at least. You'd have to travel faster than the speed of light to make such a journey in 100 years! How did you do it?"

Libra grinned. "I said . . . I traveled for 100 years . . . *in space-time,*" she answered coyly.

Cathy and Adele looked perplexed, and implored her to explain.

After a brief protest, Libra finally agreed to give them a hint. "I'll make a simple analogy," she said. "I won't be revealing too much to you, since the actual scientific explanation is a good deal more complex. Have you ever climbed a tree?"

"Y-Yes," said Cathy, with a puzzled expression. "When I was younger."

Adele nodded. "Cathy practically lived in that old oak tree on the other side of the fence," she said.

"Good," pronounced Libra with a wise smile. "Now, imagine space-time as the branches of a large tree. Voca is programmed to leap from branch to branch of space-time. It's much faster than ordinary travel."

"Amazing!" exclaimed Adele. "How was this principle ever discovered?"

Warming to the subject of Gatosian scientific history, Libra continued.

"It's quite amusing, really. Figarella, a wealthy, brilliant, and somewhat idle aristocat who lived during the Gatosian Renaissance, discovered the branch principle of space-time accidentally. According to her diary, she was contemplating the nature of the universe high up in her favorite catalpa tree when she suddenly fell. She landed with a splash in a bowl of punch that her husband, Catullus, had set out on a picnic table for their six young nieces and nephews who were visiting for the weekend. While clinging to the rim of the bowl with a twist of lemon draped over one ear she suddenly uttered her famous dictum, "Uttce ramibilus, zilchen!" which is Gatosian Latin for "Between branches, nothing!"

"That sounds like Newton and his apple, except that Figarella played the part of the apple!" laughed Cathy.

"So, if I understand you correctly, Voca is able to hop from one part of the universe to the other by leaping across . . . *space-timelessness?*" Adele queried.

Libra nodded. "Precisely. Figarella's equations predicted that it should be possible, in theory, to hop from branch to branch of space-time without ever falling, as it were, but it wasn't until Katzenheim propounded his famous 'Certainty Principle' over three hundred years later, that Figarella's law could be applied to space travel."

"Certainty Principle!" exclaimed Adele. "You mean Heisenberg was wrong? He proposed the *Un*certainty Principle."

"There's no doubt about it!" Libra answered with conviction. "Gatosian physics is all based on certainty. Otherwise, hopping from one branch of space-time to another—and landing where you want to—would be impossible!"

Cathy and Adele were astounded.

"But what about wave-particle duality? What about Schrödinger's cat?" Adele exclaimed.

"What is 'Schrödinger's cat'?" inquired Libra.

"Mother, I don't think the Commander would appreciate that story."

"Quite right, dear, I meant Schrödinger's *fish*."

"Schrödinger's *fish*?"

"Yes," said Adele. "You see, Schrödinger suggested a paradox based on the following thought experiment. Suppose you have a box divided into two chambers by a sliding door. Now suppose there's a cat in one chamber, and a fish in the other."

"Is the fish in water?" asked Libra.

"Well . . . yes, the fish is alive, so it must be in water." Adele answered.

"I see," said Libra. "Please go on."

"Now suppose there's a fifty-fifty chance that the door separating the chambers will be opened or closed," Adele continued. "But an outside observer can't tell what's going on inside the box."

"Who is the outside observer?" asked Libra.

"A person . . ." said Adele.

"I see," said Libra. "Continue."

"So the question is, is the fish alive or dead? If the door is open, the cat will get the fish and eat it. If the door is closed, the fish will survive. According to Schrödinger, since there's a fifty percent probability of either outcome, and since the observer has no way of knowing what happened inside the box, the proper interpretation is that the fish is *both* eaten *and* not eaten."

"Nonsense," said Libra.

"Nonsense?" Adele replied.

"Yes, nonsense!" said Libra. "The person may not know what happened inside the box, but the cat knows perfectly well whether or not she ate the fish!"

"Yes, but the cat doesn't count in this case," said Adele.

"*That* is the problem with Earthling physics!" declared Libra testily.

Cathy cleared her throat.

"Mother, I believe Einstein would have admired Gatosian physics," she said. "He was a great lover of certainty."

"I must say, I find Gatosian physics refreshing as well," Adele replied.

But although Adele and Cathy begged Libra to provide further details about the Certainty Principle, Libra was miffed and would say no more.

"Regulations," she kept repeating, waving their questions aside.

At last, having finished their meal, they cleared the table and adjourned to the sofa in the living room. Cathy brought out a china plate of chocolate-coated wafers and a pot of tea on a tray, along with cups and saucers for her mother and herself and a demitasse for Libra, and the conversation turned to the computer industry and then to Libra's adventures at Dogma.

"Mother," said Cathy in a hushed voice. "Libra has evidence that Jug Maraud is mixed up with Rolf Trammel, and that Maraud may be behind Daddy's death."

"That's a very serious charge, dear," Adele Cameron responded. "The police carried out a thorough investigation and found no evidence of wrong-doing." Libra noticed that Adele had averted her gaze and was biting her lower lip.

"What about Carlos Valdez? He told you that Daddy might have been forced off the road!" Cathy persisted.

"A bright and no doubt perceptive young man," replied Adele with deliberate calm. "But I trust the police, and they said—"

"But Libra heard incriminating comments at the Dogma board of directors' meeting!" Cathy interrupted.

"With all due respect to Commander Shimagrimicka," said Adele, who was becoming increasingly agitated, "she can hardly be expected to understand all the nuances of the English language, having arrived from Gatos only a few days ago. It's quite possible that she misinterpreted perfectly innocent remarks."

"Just listen to what she has to say," pleaded Cathy. "It sounds serious to me."

Adele hesitated.

"All right, Commander, what *did* you hear?" she exclaimed, turning to her diminutive guest, who had been quietly listening to the exchange while holding her demitasse in both paws on her lap.

Libra cleared her throat and replaced her cup on the glass-topped coffee table.

"Your mother's quite right," she said to Cathy. "I have no direct proof that Rolf Trammel and Jug Maraud are behind your father's death. But I'll tell you what I heard." Then, turning to Adele Cameron, Libra added, "As far as my grasp of the English language is concerned, Dr. Cameron, you needn't worry, because I have total recall. I can repeat the discussion that took place verbatim, and you can draw your own conclusions."

Cathy smiled at Libra's directness with her mother.

Having delivered her prefatory remarks, Libra then went on to relate, in exquisite detail, all that had transpired at the Dogma board of directors' meeting. Adele and Cathy both leaned forward as Libra repeated the contents of Jug Maraud's report, including the slides of the Cameron Computer building, the pictures of Felix, Adele and Cathy, and Maraud's remarks that the new technology being developed at Cameron Computers was "a threat to Dogma." Libra also quoted Jug Maraud as stating "the news ain't all bad" in referring to Dr. Cameron's death. He had also singled Cathy out as the main hindrance to Dogma's taking over Cameron Computers, and that if Adele and Cathy didn't accept Trammel's generous offer, "dey could get hoit." (Libra mimicked Maraud's New Jersey accent, which made Adele and Cathy smile in spite of the seriousness of the content.) Libra ended by noting that Mr. Trammel had invited both Jack Maraud and Frank Carne, of the Marauders motorcycle gang, into his office after the meeting to "discuss what steps should be taken."

Even as she finished, however, Libra realized that her detailed description of the meeting at Dogma contained no smoking gun. Rolf Trammel and Jug Maraud had cleverly concealed their evil intentions with irony and sarcasm, which was difficult to communicate by simply quoting their words. Libra felt frustrated.

As if echoing her thoughts, Adele Cameron stood up and began gathering up the plates, teapot and cups and placing them on the tray. "I'm sorry, Commander, but I didn't hear anything incriminating." she said. "Disgusting, perhaps, and even chilling—but not incriminating."

"But what about Jack Maraud and Frank Carne?" Cathy interjected. "They're both notorious criminals."

"I know, dear, and I'm very worried. But there's no proof. You just can't arrest people because of the company they keep. You need evidence that will hold up in court. Even if we did tell the police, how would we explain how we came by the information?" Adele quickly lifted the tray and carried it back into the kitchen, leaving Cathy and Libra alone in the living room.

"Libra, what are we going to do?" asked Cathy. "I can tell Mother's frightened, and so am I!"

"I think we should meet with Carlos Valdez as soon as possible," said Libra, after considering the matter for a moment. "It sounds as if he knows something that may be of use to us."

"We have his phone number," said Cathy. "He lives over near Salinas. He said we could call him any time if we needed him."

Peering outside through the living room window, Libra saw that evening was settling in. Streaks of gold enflamed the clouds above the horizon to the west and the shrubs on the lawn were casting long blue shadows.

"Why am I sitting here?" she exclaimed, slapping her forehead and leaping down from the sofa onto the floor. "Voca is probably frantic. She's gone several days without hearing from me. I must return immediately!"

"Can I come with you?" asked Cathy. "I'd love to meet Voca."

"Sure! Why not? Since you and your mother are going to help me to repair her, you deserve to meet her."

"How exciting! I'll get Mother. She'll want to change clothes."

"Okay," said Libra. "But hurry. I'm starting to worry— just like Voca!"

While Cathy and Adele changed into jeans and hiking shoes, Libra paced impatiently about the living room until at last her two human companions appeared, and the three of them set out along the path up the mountain and toward the meadow.

Hank and Pinny picked up the fire extinguisher and carried it up the ramp, placing it on its side in the middle of the cabin.

"I did it, Voca!" cried Pinny proudly. "I put out the fire all by myself!"

"I knew you could," said Voca. "You can do all sorts of things you never thought you could."

"I want to be a pilot, like Commander Shimagrimicka!" shrilled Pinny. She was still excited.

"Perhaps someday you will be, dear," answered Voca with just a trace of amusement in her voice. Then addressing Hank, she said: "Hank, you also demonstrated great courage in leading the motorcyclists away. I'm sure Commander Shimagrimicka will recognize you both for your bravery and for the service you've performed for the Gatosian space program."

Hank was so overcome with emotion that he didn't know what to say. He simply hung his head with a silly grin, stammered a few words of thanks in Meow, and shuffled his paws self-consciously. Pinny hopped up and down gleefully.

"According to my clock it's past your dinner time," said Voca. "You both must be hungry. How about steak and lobster tails, with all the trimmings?"

Hank nearly fainted with joy at the mention of such a sumptuous repast, and even Pinny licked her lips. The kitchen console was activated and the two cats turned to watch the blinking lights on the panel, listening curiously to the whirring, beeping and clicking noises that emanated from it.

"How do you think it works?" Pinny whispered into Hank's ear. She didn't dare ask Voca for fear of being rude.

"I don't know," Hank whispered in return, but, in fact, he wasn't much interested in how it worked, so long as it *worked*!

Nor were they disappointed in the result. A moment later two trays issued from the panel door, and brother and sister sat down to a well-earned feast. Hank dined in his usual fashion, while Pinny struggled for some time with the knife and fork, before finally giving up in exasperation and joining Hank.

Absorbed in their conversation and their meal, they failed to hear Libra, Cathy and Adele as they approached the spacecraft through the tall meadow grass.

"Looks like there's been a fire," said Cathy, pointing to the scorched grass around the ship. "But someone's put it out. See, there's foam fire retardant sprayed on the ground."

Libra bounded up the ramp and was surprised to see Hank and Pinny in the cabin, licking up the last remnants of their dinner.

"Hank! Pinny! What happened?" she cried.

"Commander Shimagrimicka!" Voca exclaimed. "You've returned! Oh, I'm so relieved! What happened to you? Are you all right? Were you being held prisoner? Did you get my new chip?"

Libra noticed with amusement the image of the calico cat on the monitor.

"Easy, Voca, one question at a time," she said, trying to calm her distraught computer. "I'm fine, although I did have a close brush with Rolf Trammel and Jug Maraud over at Dogma Computers. I'll tell you all about it later, but first let me introduce Adele Cameron, president of Cameron Computers, and her daughter Cathy. They're going to help us construct your new nanochip."

Although the exchange between Voca and Libra had been carried out entirely in Gatosian, Adele and Cathy recognized their names as they knelt on the ground outside the doorway to the spaceship, the cabin being too small to accommodate them.

"Oh, wow!" whispered Cathy to her mother as she peered inside Voca's cabin. "I can't believe this is really happening!"

"I'm very pleased to meet you," said Voca in perfect English, speaking through the virtual calico cat on the monitor. "Commander Shimagrimicka has told me a great deal about you."

"It's a great honor and a privilege for us to meet you both," said Adele Cameron, marveling at Voca's human-like personality. "We'll do everything in our power to help you and the Commander return to Gatos."

"I'll second that," exclaimed Cathy. "Don't worry, Voca, you can count on us!"

The talk continued and further amenities were exchanged until they all began to feel comfortable with one another. Libra was amused by Voca's new alter ego, the calico cat. Cathy kept staring at Hank and Pinny, who, unable to speak English, were completely left out of the conversation, although they looked intelligently from face to face.

Eventually the subject turned to the day's events at the meadow, and Voca explained to Libra how Hank and Pinny had averted a catastrophe through their courageous actions. Libra was deeply moved, and requested that the two Earthling cats recite their deeds in their own words. At first they demurred, being overcome with shyness in front of their humans, but at Libra's insistent prodding first Hank, and then Pinny, gave their versions of their encounters with the Marauders, speaking in Gatosian. And although it sounded more like rapid-fire mewing to Cathy and Adele, it was clear that Libra understood every word, since she would turn to them and translate from time to time, and they were amazed that their two adorable pets had shown such valor and could verbally communicate such a great amount of complex information.

When they had finished, Libra grew silent and seemed lost in thought. Turning to the console, she whispered something in Gatosian to Voca, and a moment later a small platform slid out from Voca's fabrication unit bearing two enameled green medallions with green velvet ribbons. Each medallion bore the image of the Great Seal of the Gatosian Republic. Libra grasped the two green medallions and then, opening a cabinet near the specimen drawers, she took out a small flagstaff with a furled flag and marched outside.

Cathy and Adele rose to their feet outside on the grass as Libra strode down the ramp, with Hank and Pinny trotting after her. They watched as Libra drove the flagstaff into the ground in the clearing just outside the spacecraft. The purple Gatosian flag, with its two penetrating green eyes set in the center of radiating yellow and black lines (which reminded Cathy of whiskers), unfurled on Earthen soil for the first time. Then, turning to the small assembled group, Libra explained that she was empowered by the Space Commission to present a distinguished Gatosian medal of honor, the Green Medallion, to non-Gatosians for acts of unusual courage in support of her mission, and that she was going to give the awards to Hank and Pinny. "I owe them a great deal, for without their help the Marauders might have found Voca," she said solemnly. "And that would have meant the end of my mission."

Speaking in Gatosian, she addressed Hank and Pinny. "Henry and Pincushion," she declared, using their formal names, "through your courage and heroism you have saved Voca from the Marauders, thereby performing an invaluable service to the Gatosian space program. By the authority vested in me by the Unified Government of the planet Gatos and the Gatosian Space Commission, it gives me great pride and pleasure to award to each of you the Green Medallion for valor. With this award also goes the eternal gratitude of every citizen of Gatos. Congratulations to you both! Leap far, land softly!"

As the evening sun sank below the horizon, it seemed to emit one final burst of crimson and gold flame, which cast purple shadows on the ground. Stepping over to the sheepish-looking Earthling cats, Libra pressed each of the medallions, which had a Velcro-like backing, onto their fur just above their hearts. Voca struck up a fanfare over the intercom, which sounded like brasses and woodwinds, followed by the Gatosian planetary anthem. As the beautiful, stately strains filled the evening air, Libra stood solemnly with her paw over her heart, watching her flag flutter in the breeze. Hank and Pinny did the same, although Hank soon wavered, lost his balance, and had to sit down. Adele and Cathy also stood at attention with their hands over their hearts, greatly moved by the honor being bestowed on their two pets. Cathy, especially, was filled with pride, and there were tears of joy streaming down her cheeks. But it was not just because Hank and Pinny were receiving this high honor. It was also because she was beginning to have hope for the future for the first time since her father's death.

Chapter 17
The Ponderosa

THE AFTERNOON WAS WARM, ALMOST HOT, and Cathy Cameron pushed back the white curtains and opened the windows over her desk. Sunlight flooded into the room, filling it with an unaccustomed brightness. A soft breeze stirred her hair and brought in the fragrance of bay laurel and madrone from the hills, together with the scent of lemon blossoms from the garden. On the fence below, the red, yellow and orange of the Matador roses shimmered in the sunshine, and the California poppies in the borders seemed impossibly bright. Strange that the rainy season had ended weeks ago, and she hadn't even noticed. Somehow she had expected it to be all gloom and drizzle outside.

She had a heavy backlog of assignments to do, but for the first time in months she felt she could cope. For the past five months she had not been able to focus on her studies at the university. Everything had seemed empty and meaningless. She had begun cutting classes and neglecting her assignments. She had bombed on several examinations, and her grades had plummeted. She had even begun toying with the idea of dropping out of school, and the more she thought about it the more sense it made to her. Instead of wasting her time taking classes she could help her mother run Cameron Computers. Her mother needed help, especially with all the problems the company was having lately. But her mother wouldn't hear of it. She insisted that Cathy had to complete her degree before working for the company. It was totally unreasonable. Her mother was just being stubborn, trying to force her to stay in school. But what good was staying in school if she was on the verge of flunking out anyway? It had made her so frustrated and angry that sometimes she had run out of the house, driven off in her car to a secluded spot in the park, and shed bitter tears.

But today, she felt, would be different. She could hardly wait to catch up on her assignments. And tonight, she and Libra would meet Carlos Valdez at the Ponderosa in Scotts Valley, and they could begin to unravel the mystery surrounding her father's death.

Stopping only once to replenish her cup of coffee, Cathy worked intently on her assignments until the light began to change and the plumed shadows of the palm trees had traversed the neighbor's fence, leaving long slanted stripes of shade across the lawn. Then she turned off her computer, arched her back, and stretched. It felt good. She had worked out a problem that had stumped her for weeks, and she knew that Professor Steinberg, who had all but given up on her, was going to be delighted.

Rising from her desk she snapped on the radio. Jack Campbell, the KTOM deejay, was dedicating a song by Amanda Shelby to Ralph in Watsonville. Cathy remembered meeting Jack at one of the dances at the Ponderosa. As she opened her closet door and examined her shirts, she listened. It was a sweet, emotional song with an old-fashioned sound that she liked. How long had it been since she had listened to the radio at home? A long time. It felt good to listen to the music, and she even wanted to wear something bright, something pretty for a change. The jeans she

Upon hearing Carlos's gloomy assessment, Cathy suddenly buried her face in her hands and sobbed. It all seemed so hopeless. How could she have been so naïve as to think that she could do more than the police to solve the mystery of her father's death? And now, Carlos was suggesting that even the police might be involved!

Reduced to the role of spectator, Libra averted her gaze to the dance floor, where smiling, boot-shod couples shuffled along in perfect synchrony, executing complex spins and turns with joined hands. Cathy's breakdown over her father's apparent murder had triggered a flood of painful memories, images of her own parents, their faces filled with love and concern as they waved to her from the VIP circle on the tarmac moments before lift-off. Then she had closed the door, forever severing her from their presence and from the life she had known. For one hundred years she had slept in her pod like a dormant seed, immune to the ravages of time. But for her mother and father back on Gatos, time had not stood still. . . .

But even as she felt tears of regret well up in her eyes, something snapped inside her. Drawing on her years of training and discipline as a member of the elite corps of Gatosian space commanders, her eyes became steely and her purpose firm once again. This was no time to be mewling like a helpless kitten! Hanging around humans was making her muddle-headed. What if some of Trammel's men were to suddenly appear? She needed all her wits about her to protect the lives of Cathy and her mother, and to successfully complete her mission.

Her eyes fastened on a particularly agile couple in their late fifties. The man was tall and lanky with a thick droopy mustache and sideburns; the lady, who was much shorter, wore a bright red dress and a silver and turquoise squash flower necklace. Libra observed that just when they seemed to have tied themselves into a knot from their gyrations, one of the partners would perform an athletic twist that would extricate them and return them to the open dance position, allowing them to move forward again. She decided it was time to intervene.

Clearing her throat, she gave Cathy a slight nudge, placed her paw on Cathy's right shoulder, and looked straight into her eyes.

"Aren't you going to introduce Carlos and me *properly,* Cathy?" she asked.

Despite his relative youth, Carlos Valdez had seen quite a lot of the world. As a boy growing up on a cattle ranch outside Las Vegas, he had learned the art of never being caught off guard, not even if a rattlesnake suddenly crawled out of his sleeping bag or if his freshly broken-in horse decided to try to wipe him off on the nearest tree. In high school he had excelled in martial arts and had done a bit of rodeoing. After graduating *magna cum laude* in criminology from the University of Nevada, he had joined the Las Vegas Sheriff's Department, where he quickly earned a reputation as a careful and meticulous investigator, with a remarkable ability to keep his cool under the most extraordinary circumstances, of which there had been plenty.

Nevertheless, when he heard Libra speak English in her small flute-like voice, Carlos nearly fell off his chair.

Cathy, distracted from her grief by Libra's sudden remark and Carlos's reaction, giggled in spite of herself.

"Carlos, allow me to introduce my 'partner in crime,' Commander Libra Shimagricka from the planet Gatos. . . ."

"Well, tomorrow should be a little less thrilling," Cathy explained, "but I think you're going to enjoy it more. We're going to meet my advisor and research supervisor, Dr. Miriam Steinberg, over at Lighthouse Point. Miriam's an expert on antimatter and the Assistant Director of SCNAC, the Santa Cruz Nonlinear Accelerator. She's also one of my father's former students and an old friend of the family. I know she'll do everything she can to help us."

"Isn't Lighthouse Point a surfing spot?" asked Libra.

"Arguably the best in Northern California!" Cathy declared. "Miriam's an avid surfer. "

Libra smiled contentedly. "Banzai," she whispered.

Chapter 19
Surf City

THE FOLLOWING DAY, A SATURDAY, Libra rendezvoused with Cathy and Adele at their house after breakfast. She showed up with a surfboard tucked under her left arm and a bright blue duffel bag hanging from her right shoulder.

"Good morning, Commander," said Cathy. "I see you're ready to hit the waves."

Libra was more than ready. She was stoked.

"This morning Voca and I watched the Steamer Lane live video cam on the Surf City website," Libra announced. "It's a perfect day, and the waves are hu*mon*gous. There was a big storm off the coast of New Zealand just a few days ago, and the south swell arrived in Santa Cruz this morning. They're predicting fifteen- to twenty-footers at the Lane."

"My! You've certainly mastered the jargon quickly," Adele remarked.

"Yes," Libra replied. "Voca downloaded the *Surfspeak Dictionary* so I could learn the local dialect."

"Well, we'd better get started," said Cathy. "We don't want to keep Miriam waiting."

Cathy strapped her green-and-white surfboard onto the roof of the H-car and loaded the rest of their things into the trunk. Adele locked the front door of the house and the three of them slid onto the front seat.

"It's funny," Cathy mused. "Normally I'd leave some extra food out for Hank and Pinny while we're away, but lately they've been spending so much time with Voca that we hardly ever see them."

"That's because Voca's been introducing them to Gatosian cuisine," remarked Libra, "although she sometimes complains that Hank eats more like a horse than a cat."

"That's our Hank!" Cathy laughed.

Cathy backed the H-car out of the driveway and they were soon heading west toward Santa Cruz. To get a better view, Libra climbed on top of the back seat and watched contentedly out the rear window. She was grinning from ear to ear and purring happily at the thought of being able to get in some surfing during her visit to Earth, especially at the thought of surfing twenty-foot waves! Imagine! As tall as a five-story building on Gatos!

"Such a glorious day!" declared Adele. "Makes me feel young again. I almost wish I could go surfing with you."

"Why don't you, Mom? You could rent a board."

"Not this trip, dear. The waves at the Lane are much too big. Besides, I'd need a wetsuit. Which reminds me— what about a wetsuit for Libra? That water's plenty cold."

"Believe it or not," said Cathy, "Libra brought her own wetsuit from Gatos. It's in her duffle bag. I put it back in the trunk with my stuff."

"Is Libra's surfboard anything like yours?"

"It's pretty sleek for a two-footer," said Cathy.

"No advanced technology?" asked Adele.

"Mom, you wouldn't believe how high-tech it is!" Cathy exclaimed. "It's got, like, all the bells and whistles, including a computerized skeg that changes angles depending on the pitch and velocity of the wave. You can program it for specific maneuvers with a toe-operated keyboard just behind the nose. It's also got hydrogen-powered jets mounted in the tail that can help you get out of tight situations, and you can do aerials even on the tiniest waves."

"I can see why you didn't just strap it onto the roof," laughed Adele.

"Yeah, makes my own board seem kinda primitive, doesn't it?" Cathy agreed.

Hearing her board being discussed, Libra hopped down from her perch by the rear window and walked onto the armrest between Cathy and Adele.

"Actually," she said, sitting down, "I have several other boards at home. Not all of them are so advanced. I use this one for acrobatics and precision surfing in contests. But most of the time I just take to the waves with the old hollow surfboard I've had ever since I was a kitten. You can't beat that feeling of freedom you get when it's just you and the waves."

"Wow, I didn't know you surfed competitively," said Cathy.

"I've been in a few contests," Libra acknowledged, obviously pleased at Cathy's interest. "The summer before I left Gatos I won third place in aerials in the Annual Purrl Beach Summer Surf Classic; the year before, I won second place in the distance event at the Miaui Aquathon."

"Miaui?"

"Miaui is a tropical island famous for its big wave surfing. It's the largest of the Feliwiian Islands, which are situated about five hundred miles offshore of Catalornia, my home province."

"You certainly showed a lot of foresight, bringing your surfboard with you all the way from Catalornia," said Adele.

"When I was a kitten at Green Eye Bay, my father used to say that I never went *anywhere* without my surfboard," smiled Libra.

They had just crested the summit when traffic suddenly came to a halt, and Cathy was forced to slam on the brakes to avoid hitting the car in front of them. Libra teetered on her perch, but quickly righted herself.

"Uh-oh," said Adele. "Looks like the usual weekend traffic jam."

"I guess we should have gotten an earlier start," sighed Cathy. "This is going to take a while."

Even though they were still at a high altitude, it was very hot outside, nearly ninety degrees. Heat waves shimmered off the roofs of the cars in front of them. Cathy turned the fan of the air-conditioner up a notch.

"Better put on a heavy layer of sunscreen," Adele said to Cathy. "You could get a real burn on a day like this."

Adele dug down into her handbag, and after feeling around found the sunscreen at the very bottom. She squeezed a small puddle of the white lotion onto the palm of her left hand and rubbed it onto her arms, neck and face. Then she passed it over to Cathy, who applied a dose to her own skin before the traffic began to inch forward again.

"I don't suppose you need any of this," Adele said, offering the bottle to Libra.

"What is it?" Libra asked

"Sunscreen," Adele replied. "It blocks out ultraviolet radiation, which causes skin cancer. Because of the widespread use of chlorofluorocarbons in spray cans and as refrigerants, the ozone layer in the atmosphere, which absorbs UV radiation, has been compromised, and the incidence of skin cancer has increased."

"Just a drop for my nose, thanks," said Libra. "Fortunately, we cats have our own natural protection against sunburn," she added, indicating her fur coat. "However, I do seem to have forgotten my sun glasses."

"Ta-da!" cried Cathy, extracting a miniature pair of sunglasses from her shirt pocket. The frames were hot pink with silver sparkles and the lenses had a bronze metallic tint. "I thought you might need some, so I brought these along. I've had them since I was a kid. They came with one of my dolls."

Libra took the glasses and held them in her paws critically. They seemed a bit garish, but she was pleased to discover that they fit her snugly and effectively cut out the sun's glare.

"Hey, cool, dude!" cried Cathy, glancing at her in the rear-view mirror.

Adele turned to see. Libra tilted her head this way and that like a fashion model. Despite their doll-sized proportions, the round lenses completely overwhelmed Libra's face.

"They make you look . . . how should I put it . . . very *California,* Commander," commented Adele dryly, suppressing a smile.

"Good," replied Libra. " I don't want to be conspicuous out there. I want to blend in."

"Don't worry," giggled Cathy, "they'll just think you're from L. A."

Cathy turned and extended her forefinger bearing a small white dab of sunscreen

"Now hold still, Commander, while I put some lotion on your nose."

During their slow, winding passage through the Santa Cruz Mountains, Cathy drilled Libra on the argot of the local surfers, in case one of them should strike up a conversation with her. She explained the various forms of address, such as "Hey, dude!" and "Howzit, bro?," and how to tell the difference between an insult and a compliment, which wasn't always easy. Libra was surprised how many different words there were to describe waves, like glassy, tubular, gnarly, and mackin'.

"It's called 'mackin' ' because it hits you like a Mack truck . . . kablam!" said Cathy. "In surfspeak, you say you 'got splampted by an insanely hairball behemoth!'"

"Bit-chin'!" Libra replied. "I'd rather wipe out in a mackin' triple overhead, than wallow all day in burgery smurf!" she improvised.

"Bravo!" cried Adele.

"Awesome, Commander!" Cathy exclaimed. "You're a natural-born surfer dude."

Libra purred audibly.

"You seem to have quite a flair for this, Commander," remarked Adele. "Do Gatosian surfers have their own dialect as well?"

"No, we have nothing like surfspeak back in Catalornia," Libra replied wistfully. "Feliwiian surfers have coined a phrase or two, but they're pretty tame by Earth standards. For example, when you get knocked over by a wave, it's called being 'licked by big mother.' "

"How sweet!" said Cathy. "That's so sweet!"

"Yes," sighed Libra, with a look of chagrin. "Cats as a rule tend to be somewhat reserved when it comes to expressing themselves. Mind you, I'm not your typical Gatosian. I like a colorful turn of phrase. One of the first things I intend to do when I get back to Gatos is to introduce California surfing terms in Catalornia. It would certainly enrich our vocabulary."

They passed by the Scotts Valley exit that Cathy and Libra had taken the previous night on their way to the Ponderosa, and continued toward the coast. At length they arrived at the first traffic light of the town of Santa Cruz and came to a halt. To the right Libra spotted what looked like a building supply company. The backyard was a mosaic of neatly piled stones, bricks and cinderblocks of various shapes, sizes and colors. To the left she noticed a greyish, rather nondescript shopping mall—much smaller than the one she had visited in San Jose.

The light changed and they drove up Mission Street to Bay, then turned left. They passed by a residential neighborhood on the right, and a huge water treatment

plant on the left, eventually ending at West Cliff Drive.
Before them loomed the large, gray rectangular edifice of
the West Coast Santa Cruz Hotel, built on the cliff overlooking the beach and boardwalk. The huge monolithic
structure, which had been erected before the Coastal
Commission was appointed, eclipsed the view of the bay
entirely.

Turning right onto West Cliff Drive, they passed the
more modest Sea and Sand Motel on the left, and got their
first peek at Monterey Bay. On the near shore, novice sail-
boarders struggled with their awkward craft in the shal-
low waves, straining to keep their multi-colored sails aloft.
Directly behind, the Municipal Wharf jutted out to sea
with its load of restaurants and touristic gift shops and its
subsurface burden of fish-fattened sea lions lounging on
the cross-beams among the pilings. Off in the distance,
sailboats plied the deeper waters and a fringe of white sand
beach curved around and headed westward toward the town
of Monterey, disappearing finally in the afternoon haze.

Libra noticed that the beach beyond the wharf was
crowded with bathers in swimsuits and that there was a
boardwalk directly behind it peopled with strollers. The
boardwalk was connected to a harlequin-painted structure
that resembled the exposed inner workings of a vast
machine with its giant cogs spinning, swinging, swooping
and tilting in the sunlight.

"What's that?" Libra asked, pointing at the huge
assemblage of colorful moving parts.

"Oh, that's the Santa Cruz Beach Boardwalk,"
answered Cathy. "It's an amusement park. They have rides
and stuff. Some of them are pretty scary, but it's a lot of
fun."

The exaggerated screams of determined vacationers
could be heard ricocheting off the water, mingling with the
raucous cries of seagulls wheeling overhead in their endless search for tidbits.

"Are there amusement parks on Gatos?" asked Adele.

"Of course," said Libra, not to be outdone. "Not so large, perhaps. . . ."

"I'll bet Pinny would love to ride on a roller coaster," Cathy speculated, imagining her little tabby cat frolicking with others of her kind at a Gatosian amusement park. "Hank, on the other hand . . ." She hesitated. "Well, he *used* to be timid. But ever since he met you and Voca he's become a lot bolder. Maybe he'd enjoy it, too."

"I don't care much for amusement parks, myself," sniffed Libra. "Although I suppose I ought to try it out— should the occasion present itself—in order to report back to the Space Commission."

"I'm afraid we won't have time for that today, Commander," smiled Adele.

"Oh . . . right," said Libra, obviously crestfallen.

They wound along West Cliff Drive, passing several lovely Victorian houses on their right, some of them enormous even by Earth standards. At a stop sign on Pelton Avenue just outside Lighthouse Field, they paused to gaze at a bronze sculpture of a surfer. He stood with his arms extended backwards, grasping the sides of a longboard, which rose like an obelisk behind him. His face was turned to the left toward Lighthouse Point, his yearning gaze fixed upon the waves of Steamer Lane. The statue was surrounded by beds of flowers with a reddish gravel path and a pair of benches for the foot-weary stroller. A flower lei had been placed around the surfer's neck by an admirer, and a dedication—"To All the Surfers Who Have Caught Their Last Wave"—was engraved on one of the benches.

"That's a statue honoring the longboarders, the surfers who first started surfing at Steamer Lane in the 1940s and '50s," explained Cathy. "Not many people use longboards anymore. They're not very maneuverable compared to miniboards."

"I thought maybe it was for group surfing," said Libra. "In Gatos, we have team surfboard events, where five to ten surfers will ride on the same board. Some of the team boards are almost as long as that longboard."

"I've heard of tandem surfing by couples," said Cathy, "but team surfing sounds much more difficult."

"It requires a great deal of cooperation and practice," answered Libra. "Adults regard it as a salutary discipline for youth, because it forces them to function as a unit—something that doesn't come naturally to kittens. I confess that team surfing was my least favorite water sport at summer camp."

The car behind them honked, and Adele drove on. A short distance away she turned into the parking lot across the street from Lighthouse Point.

"We're here at last!" she announced, shutting off the engine.

The doors of the H-car swung open and all three trundled out, stretching their arms and legs after the hour-long journey.

"There's Miriam's car," said Cathy, pointing to an old-model ethanol-electric hybrid a few cars away. "Looks like she's already out in the water."

Adele popped open the trunk with the remote on her keychain. Cathy reached in, unzipped her duffel bag and handed Libra her wetsuit, which was constructed of an unfamiliar lightweight, foamy fabric with a metallic luster that glittered in the sunlight like gold lamé.

"That's really dazzling, Commander," remarked Adele. "What kind of material is it? I've never seen anything like it."

"My wetsuit? Oh, it's made of an advanced . . . hmmm . . . sorry, Adele, I really shouldn't say."

"*Mo-ther!*" scolded Cathy. "You know about Space Academy regulations!"

"I'm sure the Commander, as a fellow scientist, will forgive my curiosity," Adele replied hastily.

"It's only natural," Libra smiled tolerantly, and the subject was quickly dropped.

Since Cathy was wearing her swimsuit under her clothes, she changed into her wetsuit right there on the parking lot beside the car. She made Libra change in the car, however, so as not to attract attention. While Libra slipped into her wetsuit, Cathy unfastened her surfboard from the car roof. Then she slid it gently down to the asphalt surface and leaned it against the side of the H-car, just as Libra emerged from the back door.

"You look great, Commander . . ."

"Thanks!" said Libra, adjusting her sunglasses.

". . . but your right ear is poking out," Cathy added.

Libra glanced up. "Oops," she said, pulling her hood down over the errant ear. "I usually don't wear the hood. I'm afraid it's a little small."

Just then four laughing, tow-headed, barefooted teenagers in black neoprene wetsuits walked by still dripping from the surf, with their surfboards tucked loosely under their arms.

"Bucket o' nugs, dude, I'm stoked!" exclaimed the tallest boy to his friends while grinning a toothy grin.

"Twenty-foot corduroy to the hor-i-zen, and pumping!" observed a thin, freckle-faced boy with large ears that bent out from his head like scallop shells.

"Way rad killer surf—off the Richter!" piped the third boy. From the shape and angle of his ears, he might have been the second boy's younger brother. "Did you see me clocking in the green room? It was sacred, dude."

"I ate it somethin' fierce on that last closeout!" the first boy chimed in, seeming to relish his own hydraulic destruction.

"Hey, dudes, let's jet over to the Wiki-Chicki and get some nuggets and shakes before it gets all zoo'ed out down there," exclaimed the fourth surfer, a girl with a badly sun-burned nose and sodden, shoulder-length hair. She was staring straight at Cathy and Libra.

"Stokaboka!" agreed the freckle-faced boy, as they abruptly ended their conversation and streaked toward an ancient, beat-up station wagon at the far end of the lot.

Cathy glanced down at her friend and saw that she was mesmerized by the young surfers.

"Commander?"

"Where's my board?" Libra suddenly blurted out as if in a trance.

"It's in the trunk," answered Cathy.

In an instant, Libra had plucked her surfboard from its wrapping of beach towels. She ran her right paw over the rail, feeling its smoothness. The silvery board glinted in the sun like a mirror.

"Wax?" she asked.

"Here," said Cathy, handing her a bar.

With a few practiced strokes, Libra waxed the upper surface of her board, all two feet of it.

"It's important to coat the whole length of the board," Libra explained to Adele, "especially if you do acrobatics. Otherwise you can slip off."

"I'll remember that," laughed Adele, "although there's not much chance I'll be doing any acrobatics, surfing or otherwise."

"I'm ready!" Libra announced, stuffing the small bar into a pocket designed for that purpose on the front of her wetsuit.

"Me, too!" Cathy answered, putting the finishing touches on her own board. Libra's excitement was infectious. "Let's go!" she cried out.

Adele retrieved her purse from the back seat, closed the doors to the H-car and locked them with the remote, and the three of them walked briskly out of the parking lot toward the wooden stairs that led down the cliff to the water. Overhead, a solitary plane towed a fluttering banner across the cloudless sky: "Welcome to Surf City."

They passed by a brick lighthouse on the right and approached the top of the stairway. From here Libra could see the whitecaps of the tallest waves, and her whole body tingled with anticipation. They pushed their way through the crowd of curious passersby who had paused to watch the action. The spectators leaned excitedly over the aluminum railing along the cliff top, exclaiming over each gigantic wave.

"Whoa! Look at that one!" cried a long-haired young man in a blue O'Neill's t-shirt and shorts.

"Twenty feet, at least!" marveled a middle-aged woman in a jogging suit.

"Awesome!" murmured a gap-toothed girl in a wetsuit, seated on a bicycle.

Libra's eyes opened wide as she viewed the wave front for the first time. They were on a scale beyond her wildest imaginings, and the pounding of the surf was deafening. On Gatos, each one of these watery goliaths would be considered a tidal wave, capable of washing out whole villages. Surfing such waves was the opportunity of a lifetime, and made the hundred-year voyage to Earth seem worth every second.

Wasting no time, Cathy and Libra quickly descended the stairs and stepped carefully onto the rocks that lined the cliff. As they eased their way toward the water's edge, one of the spectators, a young blond-haired man sporting a red floral Hawaiian shirt and sipping a soft drink from a can, suddenly blurted out, "Hey, get a load of the kid in the gold wetsuit and the pink shades!"

All heads turned toward Libra, who was too focused on the waves to notice the attention she was drawing.

"Wow, the metallic finish on that surfboard really sparkles," said a girl of about sixteen, as she aimed her camera at Libra and clicked away.

"Real flashy," agreed an elderly gentleman wearing a straw hat. "Got to be from L. A."

"Yeah, he's not a local, that's for sure. I know just about every kid who surfs the Lane, and I never seen him before," said a twelve-year-old boy in a wetsuit, perched on the railing..

"I don't think it's a kid," opined a thin young woman with a pony tail. She had been running along West Cliff Drive and was now jogging in place in order to keep up her heart rate while watching the waves. "Looks more like a really small midget to me."

There followed a discussion about whether Libra was a child or a midget.

Adele, overhearing their remarks, became concerned that Libra was far too conspicuous, but speculations about Libra's identity soon subsided and she was accepted as just another eccentric surfer from the south. A fresh set of gargantuan breakers, as tall as housetops, garnered the attention of the spectators, and Adele began to relax.

As she stepped off the last boulder, Cathy eased onto her surfboard and paddled out to where the waves were breaking. Libra followed close behind.

"Let's go out to the line-up," said Cathy. "I think I see Miriam out there."

Miriam Steinberg was sitting astride her board, staring intently at the incoming sets.

"Hi, Miriam! We're over here!" Cathy shouted.

"Cathy! Wait—here comes my wave!"

Miriam rotated towards the shore and proned out on her board just ahead of a huge breaker. At the critical moment, she stood up and began to carve up and down the vertical face just ahead of the curling lip, working her board back and forth with powerful thrusts of her legs to extract every ounce of momentum from the wave. Cathy and Libra floated over the smooth swell of Miriam's wave and sank gently down into the trough. For a few moments

Miriam was hidden from view by the bank of whitewater that pursued her toward the shore. Then they caught sight of her again as she peeled off the now-tamed shoulder, to the enthusiastic applause of the spectators on the cliff.

"Here comes another big one," Cathy exclaimed. "I'm going to try to catch it!"

The wave was approaching like a freight train. Cathy turned toward shore and began paddling furiously. Libra watched anxiously as the huge wave broke over Cathy, and her friend disappeared under a curved wall of coursing green water. Suddenly, Cathy emerged from the leading edge of the tube like a butterfly from its chrysalis, wet and folded for minimum resistance. Shouts and cheers from the spectators wafted down from the cliffs. To show off for Miriam and Libra, Cathy performed a couple of cutbacks into the crests before coasting to a stop some hundred meters away from her starting point.

"Great ride," said Miriam, when they had both returned to the line-up.

"Thanks!" replied Cathy. "Those waves are fantastic!"

"Maybe we should get in some more surfing before we talk shop," said Miriam.

"Agreed," replied Cathy.

Just then their attention was diverted by the sound of ooohs and ahhhs emanating not only from the cliffs, but from the surfers in the water as well.

"Geez!" exclaimed a surfer nearby. "Now that's what I call hot-dogging!"

"I don't believe this!" declared another young surfer.

Turning toward the incoming wave, Cathy and Miriam saw a great translucent tunnel, and inside the glassy tube was a surfer wearing a gold lamé wet suit doing 360-degree turns inside it. Round and round she went in corkscrew fashion, keeping just ahead of the collapsing wall of thundering whitewater, which seemed to be chasing her with gaping jaws like a great white shark.

But from Libra's vantage point within the green cathedral of water, all was eerily calm and quiet. She could just make out the muffled roar of the crowd and the shouts of encouragement that reached her from the secular world outside.

"Cowabunga!" she yelled. "If only Voca could see me now!"

Pulling out all the stops, she cut back and reversed the direction of her spiral. Then, just before close-out, she deftly spun out of the tube, did a somersault in mid-air while holding onto her surfboard with her right paw, and landed softly on the exhausted giant's depleted shoulder as it shrugged past her toward the rocks.

The crowd assembled on the cliffs, which had quickly grown to a mob, erupted in frenzied applause. Even the most jaded and well-traveled of her fellow surfers joined in. Several of them paddled over to her and shook her paw.

"Unreal ride, bro!" one said in reverent tones.

"Mythic, dude!" chimed in another.

"Outta control!"

"Outrageous to the max!"

At her return to the line-up, Cathy and Miriam paddled over to Libra's side.

"That was quite an exhibition," said Miriam. "If I hadn't seen it with my own eyes I wouldn't have believed it. You may have even broken some of the laws of physics! Where did you learn to surf like that?"

Libra looked at Cathy, and Cathy cleared her throat. As the other surfers had disbanded and were busily catching waves—some of them trying Libra's corkscrew maneuver with disastrous results—Cathy decided it was safe to break the news to Miriam.

"Well, you see, Miriam, Libra is from—"

She had barely uttered the words, "the planet Gatos," when they heard the shrill whine of engines and looked up to see two Jet Skis bearing down on them. The drivers were hooded and wore large goggles, but Cathy instantly recognized the handlebar mustache of Frank Carne. She also recognized his nasty-looking partner with the scraggly red beard, a man named "Hog," from the brawl at the Ponderosa. They were only thirty meters away and closing fast. The other surfers protested and gesticulated loudly, but to no avail, as the two men tore through the waves.

A cry of alarm went up from the bystanders on the cliff.

"Watch out!" one of the surfers shouted. "They're trying to run you down!"

"Dive!" cried Miriam. All three dove beneath the waves, just as the two Jet Skis crashed into their surfboards. For a few seconds the Jet Skiers made small circles over the spot where the surfers had gone down. Then they turned away and headed out to sea, where a large speedboat awaited their return.

Chapter 20
Confab at Aldo's

THE ASSEMBLED SPECTATORS ON THE CLIFF overlooking Steamer Lane, especially Adele, held their collective breath as the Jet Skis bore down on the surfers, and an audible sigh of relief went up as Cathy, Miriam and Libra surfaced from their dives unharmed.

Relief was followed quickly by anger.

"That was criminal!"

"Those maniacs tried to kill those surfers!"

"Somebody call the cops!"

"Anybody got a cell phone?"

"I've got one!"

"Call 911!"

Adele became alarmed. If the authorities were summoned and began asking questions, it would be difficult to conceal Libra's identity, and who knows what would happen once the government and the military became aware of Voca's existence? They would almost certainly confiscate her in the name of national security, and then the scientists would want to take her apart in order to understand her technology. This would not only terminate Voca's mental functions and jeopardize the Commander's return to Gatos, but it would also violate the prime directive of the

Gatosian Space Commission. For as much as Adele herself would have loved to learn all about Gatosian technology and Voca's circuitry, she was unwilling to compromise Libra's mission in order to do so.

"Hurry, Cathy, hurry!" Adele murmured under her breath.

On the positive side, the Jet Ski incident had served to divert attention away from Libra. Indeed, Libra's feats of athleticism were quickly forgotten in the wake of the Jet Skis' murderous rampage as all attention shifted to outrage at their plight.

As soon as she broke the surface, Cathy looked around to see whether Miriam and Libra were all right. A moment later, Miriam, popped up beside her, and then Libra a short distance away.

"That was close!" Miriam sputtered, gasping for air. "Who were they? Friends of yours?"

"Friends of Rolf Trammel, I'm afraid," Cathy replied anxiously.

"Well, whoever they are," Miriam continued, "they really did a number on my surfboard. The right side is completely crushed…"

"Yeah, mine's dinged up pretty badly, too!" Glancing up at the cliff, Cathy saw her mother gesturing frantically. "We'd better get out of here. Someone's bound to call the police, and that would be extremely awkward."

Libra, who had seriously considered chasing after the two Jet Skiers using her hydrogen-powered surfboard, but had wisely decided against it, paddled over to Cathy and Miriam. Her hood had fallen back, exposing her ears.

"Are you okay?" she asked.

"Sure, just a little shaken up," replied Cathy. "Mother's calling us back to shore. We'd better go immediately."

Miriam stared at Libra in amazement.

"Aren't you a *cat?*" she asked incredulously.

"Yes—from the planet Gatos, on the other side of the galaxy—I'll explain later," was Libra's terse reply. She readjusted her hood and tucked in her ears.

As they paddled back to shore, their fellow surfers escorted them, calling out words of sympathy and mutual outrage over the unprovoked Jet Ski assault. Cathy and Miriam thanked them for their support, politely refusing all offers of aid as they climbed the stairs.

Adele met them at the head of the staircase.

"We've got to get away from here! The police will be here soon, and we can't have them interviewing Libra!" she whispered.

No sooner had Libra's back paws touched the sidewalk when she was accosted by a young man with a large camera dangling from his neck and a tape recorder in his hand.

"Hi! I'm Sebastian Gale, reporter for the online surfing magazine *Mav Surfer!*" he said. "Any comments about your ride today? You've just taken the sport of surfing to a new level, dude! Those 360-degree turns inside the tube were unbelievable! I'd like to do a feature article about you. Would you be willing to take your act to Mavericks? We're talking big time—endorsements, movie contracts, book royalties, a whole new line of surfboards and wetsuits, you name it!"

Libra's eyes opened wide, and she managed to speak only one word—"Mavericks?"—before Cathy intervened.

"Thank you very much, Mr. Gale, but we really must be going."

"Can I at least get your name—?"

"Good-bye, Mr. Gale!" Adele interposed in a stern motherly voice.

Cathy, who was standing behind Libra, placed her hands on Libra's shoulders and gently steered her across the street. The frustrated young reporter grumbled, kicked a nearby trashcan, and turned away in chagrin.

Having extricated Libra from the reporter's verbal tentacles, they made their way quickly to the parking lot.

"Why don't you grab your things and come with us?" Cathy said to Miriam. "We can talk while driving."

Miriam readily agreed and retrieved her clothes from the front seat of her car. Adele slid behind the wheel of the H-car and popped open the trunk. While Cathy and Miriam secured the two damaged surfboards to the car roof, Libra wrapped her own board, which was unharmed, in a beach towel and placed it in the trunk. Cathy then pushed down on the lid, which was too high for Libra to reach, and all three piled into the H-car without even bothering to change out of their wetsuits.

"There goes the upholstery!" Adele complained mildly, as she drove out of the parking lot onto West Cliff Drive.

"Don't worry, Mom. We're sitting on towels."

"Where shall we go?" Adele asked.

"How about Aldo's?" suggested Cathy.

"Sounds good to me!" Miriam agreed.

"Aldo's it is!" Adele declared, steering the H-car towards the yacht harbor, just as three police cars were converging on Steamer Lane.

Having successfully avoided an encounter with the police, they returned to the business at hand. Miriam, bursting with curiosity about Libra, demanded to hear the whole story, so Cathy related Libra's adventures from the beginning.

At first Miriam was nonplussed and skeptical about Libra's identity, but like most theoretical physicists she kept an open mind.

"I'm delighted to meet you, Commander," she said, "but I have to confess that I'm not yet convinced you are who you say you are—that is, a cat from another planet—although you certainly seem to be a cat, which is remarkable in its own right, since we're having this conversation. Oh dear. Am I making any sense?"

"I appreciate your caution completely, Dr. Steinberg," replied Libra. "As a scientist myself I always reserve judgment until the evidence is conclusive. I wish we could be meeting under less trying circumstances. But as Cathy says, the situation is urgent."

They had arrived at the top of the hill overlooking the yacht harbor. Adele found a parking space on a nearby street and they got out of the car. They could see a crowd of people gathered at the entrance to Aldo's Restaurant waiting to be seated. They walked down the hill together, and Adele got in line for a table. Cathy, Miriam and Libra, who were still in their wetsuits, headed for a public shower and changing room located a short distance away along the esplanade, where rows of yachts tethered in their slips rocked gently in the cobalt blue water. They peeled off their wetsuits and took turns showering. Although the shower seemed more like a torrential downpour to Libra, she was glad to be able to wash the salt out of her fur. While Cathy and Miriam changed back into their street clothes, Libra dried her fur with a dishtowel Cathy had brought along expressly for that purpose. She was in the midst of drying her back in the usual fashion, standing up on her hind paws and vigorously pulling the towel from side to side behind her, when a woman entering the facility spotted her.

"What's *that?*" she shrieked.

Fortunately, Cathy was close by and was able to quickly throw her own towel on top of Libra, shielding her from view. Then, drawing her onto her lap, she began rubbing Libra as if she were an ordinary Earthling cat who had just had a bath.

"It's just my cat," explained Cathy. "She fell off the dock into the water."

Libra was mortified on two accounts: because of the indignity of being dried by someone else, and at the ridiculous notion that she would fall off the dock. But she understood the need for deception and so held her temper in check.

The woman did a double-take.

"That's funny, for a moment I thought . . ."

"Anything wrong?" Cathy inquired.

The woman rubbed her eyes.

"For a moment I thought . . . but I must have been hallucinating!"

"Would you like to sit down?" Miriam, who had witnessed the incident, asked solicitously.

"No, thanks, I'm all right. It must be the sun," the woman answered. Still disconcerted, she gave them a strange look and abruptly exited the facility. Cathy and Miriam breathed a sigh of relief.

Libra finished drying by standing under the hand blow-drier, and combed her coat while Cathy and Miriam stood watch at the door. Having narrowly avoided detection, they returned to the H-car to stow their wetsuits, with Libra being careful to walk on all fours. By the time they returned to the restaurant, Adele was already seated at a table.

Aldo's Restaurant, located near the mouth of the yacht harbor, was a small building with a large wooden deck perched over the water on redwood pilings sunk deep into the sandy bottom. Adele had chosen a table next to the outer railing. From here diners could watch the gleaming yachts and colorful sailboats as they glided past on their way in or out of the harbor. Libra sat upright in Cathy's lap, with her head just above the table top, trying not to attract attention. Cathy unfolded the menu and held it upright in front of her, allowing Libra to make her selection unnoticed. After Cathy rejected her first choice, a shrimp Louie, because it would require her to use a fork, Libra settled on fish and chips.

When the waitress had finished taking their orders, Miriam leaned across the table with her fingers interlaced before her.

"Okay," began Miriam. "You've told me the story of how Libra came here and about Voca's damaged chip. Now let's just assume that everything you've told me is true and accurate. It's still not clear to me what I can do to help you. You're going to have to go into a little more detail on the technical aspects. What kind of chip are we talking about anyway?"

All eyes turned to Libra.

"It just your basic superconducting-furry logic-anti-matter-power interface nanochip with quantum gravity switches," Libra explained.

"Whew, that doesn't sound 'basic' to me!" exclaimed Miriam. "I'm going to have to ask a few questions. For starters, what's furry logic? I know what *fuzzy* logic is, but I've never heard of *furry* logic."

"Furry logic is like fuzzy logic, only more so," answered Libra.

"I see . . ." Miriam replied tentatively. "And what about the anti-matter? What type of anti-matter do you need?"

"Screechium," Libra replied.

"Screechium?"

Just then the waitress returned and dragged over a small metal stand for her tray. Libra paused as the young woman placed their plates and bottles of tea before them. Miriam had ordered Belgian waffles with fresh strawberries and whipped cream, Cathy had a mushroom and cheese omelette, Adele had a club sandwich and cole slaw, and Libra had fish and chips. The waitress departed and Libra resumed.

"Yes, it's in group thirteen of the periodic table of anti-matter elements. It's the anti-matter version of ummanumium, a transition metal."

"An anti-matter transition metal element?"

"Precisely," declared Libra, unobtrusively taking a bite out of one of her chips.

"Aren't anti-matter elements dangerous?" asked Miriam.

"Not when stabilized in a quasi-matter matrix. Luckily, quasi-matter is a natural byproduct of screechium production. . . ."

"Commander," interrupted Adele, "would you like a little catsup on your fish and chips?" Libra looked puzzled, so Adele poured a little puddle of the thick red condiment from a bottle onto her plate, next to the chips. Libra dipped her fish into the catsup and took another bite.

"Not bad," she pronounced.

"Commander," Miriam continued. "Anti-matter elements and quasi-matter are way beyond our physics on Earth. We have anti-matter subatomic particles, but not entire atoms. However, I'm beginning to understand why Adele and Cathy set up this meeting. I suppose they've told you that I'm assistant director at the Santa Cruz Nonlinear Accelerator."

"Yes," replied Libra. "That's why we're here."

"The Santa Cruz Nonlinear Accelerator, or SCNAC for short, is the top antimatter laboratory in the world, and probably the only facility that can possibly help you make screechium. Since the research at SCNAC is top secret, I'm not supposed to talk about it. However, Gatosian physics is so far ahead of Earthling physics, I don't think I could tell you anything you don't already know. We're the ones who stand to learn something from you."

Libra nodded.

"As assistant director, I can get you into the facility, and I can try to persuade Howard Ng, the director, to go along with the project, but he makes the final decision. There are a lot of projects queued up ahead of you."

"But this is a very unusual situation, Miriam," Adele emphasized. "How often do we get the opportunity to collaborate on a research project with a visitor from another planet?"

"I realize that," Miriam responded, "but you wouldn't believe some of the egos at SCNAC. I mean, they wouldn't even let E. T. go ahead of them, let alone Libra, who looks just like an ordinary Earthling cat. I'll do everything in my power, of course, but as I said, the final decision rests with Howard Ng."

"Howard Ng was a good friend of Cathy's father, Felix," Adele remarked. "He may agree to help as a personal favor to Cathy and me."

"There's one more issue, Commander," Miriam continued, dragging the last piece of Belgian waffle through the remains of whipped cream and maple syrup on her plate. "Even if we succeed in making screechium, how are you going to incorporate it into a nanochip? That's not something we can help you with at SCNAC." She turned to Adele. "That's more in your line of work, isn't it, Adele?"

'That's right, Miriam. This is a perfect opportunity to try out our new Feynmanator at Mountain View. "

"Feynmanator?" asked Libra. "I've never heard of it."

"It's probably too new to be included in any of the databases that Voca downloaded," Adele answered. "The Feynmanator was specifically designed to print molecular circuits onto nanochips. We've run it through some tests, but we haven't actually made an entire chip yet."

"Okay," said Miriam, "let's summarize. Assuming Dr. Ng gives the go ahead, Libra will direct the experiment to produce screechium at SCNAC. Once you have the screechium, you'll transport it to UC Santa Cruz's Mountain View campus and use the Feynmanator to print the circuits and quantum gravity switches onto the nanochip."

"Sounds like a plan," Cathy agreed.

"There's just one other problem," said Libra.

"What's that?" asked Cathy.

"I need to access Voca's database in order to download the schematics for the circuitry into the Feynmanator.

Unfortunately, I've lost my communicator . . . but if I had a cell phone, I believe I could modify it to contact Voca."

"You can use mine," said Adele, handing Libra a small rectangular object made of black plastic, similar to the one she had opened up at the phone store.

Libra took it in her paw and examined it. "A screwdriver and a few other tool would make it easier," she said. "Back in the city I tried to modify one of these using my claws, but I never got to finish the job."

"The Feynmanator facility has a complete tool shop," said Adele.

"Good," Libra replied, handing the phone back to Adele. "I'll borrow this from you when we're ready to download."

"We'd better get started immediately," said Cathy. "There's not a moment to lose. Rolf Trammel and the Marauders will stop at nothing—and Libra, mother, and I are tops on their hit list!"

The waitress brought them their check, and Adele took care of the bill.

During the drive back to the Lighthouse Point parking lot at Steamer Lane, Libra entertained Miriam, Cathy and Adele with stories about growing up on Gatos. Just as they were pulling into the parking lot at Steamer Lane, Cathy broke the news to them that she would not be going to SCNAC.

"Why not, dear?" her mother asked.

"Let's just say I have an important date with a certain private detective," she smiled mysteriously.

"I hope he's good-looking," laughed Miriam.

Cathy surprised herself by blushing.

"It's not that kind of date, Miriam," she protested, blushing even further.

Since Cathy needed the car to return to Los Gatos, it was agreed that Libra and Adele would go with Miriam in her car to SCNAC. Once the screechium was produced,

Miriam would deliver Libra, Adele and the screechium to the U. C. Santa Cruz campus in Mountain View.

"I haven't seen the Feynmanator yet," Miriam said. "Besides, I want to know how all of this is going to turn out. Perhaps the Commander would even introduce me to Voca."

"I'd be happy to," Libra replied. "Voca's very sociable, and she loves to talk about science. I'm sure she'd enjoy your company."

"A sociable computer!" Miriam exclaimed. "Sounds like science fiction!"

Miriam got out of the H-car, followed by Adele and Libra, and Cathy slid behind the wheel.

"Please be careful, dear!" said Adele, giving Cathy a hug through the open window.

"Don't worry, Mom. I'll be fine. It's just something I've got to do. Bye, Miriam! Bye, Commander! I'll see you later!"

Cathy pulled out of the parking lot and turned in the direction of Bay Street. A few minutes later, the old hybrid sedan—with Miriam, Adele, and Libra on the front seat—backed out of its parking space to began the climb uphill towards the U. C. Santa Cruz campus and SCNAC.

Chapter 21
Beneath Scrawny's Tree

SCNAC, THE UNIVERSITY OF CALIFORNIA NONLINEAR ACCELERATOR, was a labyrinthine underground structure lodged deep in the redwood forest behind the U. C. Santa Cruz campus proper. The site was chosen because the natural limestone caves, which penetrated the subsurface area like giant wormholes, were easily converted into the extensive maze of curving shafts that the nonlinear accelerator required. The main entrance to SCNAC was located in the basement of the physics building. After passing through a series of security clearance checkpoints, workers took an underground tram that deposited them at the entrance to the facility itself somewhere beneath the sprawling two-thousand-acre grounds of the U. C. Santa Cruz campus.

However, the laboratory also had a secret "back door" entrance, known only to those with security clearances, which was gained by entering the hollow trunk of an enormous redwood tree deep in the forest. This tree was the sole survivor of the original forest that had been clear-cut back in the early 1900s to fuel the limestone kilns that still dotted the campus. Much of the lime that had been produced here had been shipped to San Francisco to make the concrete that was needed to rebuild the city after the devastating earthquake of 1906. This sole redwood tree had been spared for one reason and one reason alone: a cat (it was a beat-up old orange tabby named Scrawny) belonging to the ranch owner's daughter had climbed into the uppermost branches of the tree and had refused to come down. Melissa Sprowell, then only ten years old, had raised such a fuss that her father had intervened and the tree was spared. Scrawny stayed up in that tree for a long time, taking all his meals there for weeks, and by the time he did come down, the lumbermen had cleared the area and moved on to another sector. And they never went back. From then on Melissa always referred to the venerable redwood as "Scrawny's Tree."

It was just as well the lumbermen spared Scrawny's Tree, since it was almost completely hollow and therefore worthless as timber. One entered the wide hogan of its trunk by slipping through a crevice, an old scar left over from a lightning strike that predated Melissa or even the Sprowell family ranch itself by many hundreds of years. Once inside, it was possible to see to the top of the tree through a breach in the upper portion of the trunk. Here sunlight filtered down into the perfumed darkness of the damp inner walls and made one feel quiet and still and content. Melissa had come here often with Scrawny, and that is why Scrawny had selected this particular tree to climb when the loggers had arrived with their saws and axes. Since that time the forest had grown back from stump sprouts, as redwoods will do, and Scrawny's tree was once again surrounded by a thick forest, albeit composed of mere toddlers compared to itself. Much later, when Melissa Sprowell donated the ranch to the University of California, she could hardly have anticipated that one day a chancellor of the university would select Scrawny's tree as the secret back entrance to SCNAC. The primary purpose of the back door, as mandated by safety regulations, was to serve as an alternative means of escape during emergencies, such as fires, earthquakes, or injuries to the staff. However, the director and assistant director were authorized to use the back door as an entrance as well, when the urgency of a situation justified by-passing normal security checks.

Many of the experiments carried out at SCNAC were of an obscure theoretical nature. However, the primary mission of the facility, for which it received the bulk of its funding from the Department of Energy, was to produce an anti-matter ray or beam that could convert highly danger-ous radioactive isotopes into harmless non-radioactive ele-ments, thus providing a safe method for disposing of radioactive waste. This mission was highly classified and entirely unknown except to a few of SCNAC's top scien-tists. U. C. Santa Cruz had been selected as the site for the facility through the foresight of the Santa Cruz City Council, which had long before designated Santa Cruz as a "nuclear-free zone." Coincidentally, U. C. Santa Cruz had become the world's center for nonlinear thinking of all kinds, and screechium, which is an anti-matter element, can only be produced by a nonlinear accelerator. Libra was therefore fortunate indeed that Voca had chosen to land near Santa Cruz, the site of the only nonlinear accelerator in the world.

As they drove up the hill toward campus, Miriam told the story of Scrawny's tree and the building of SCNAC, and as she expected, Libra took a personal interest in Scrawny.

"I would like to have met old Scrawny," she said. "Cats have marvelous powers of intuition, and some cats are clairvoyant. I wouldn't be surprised if Scrawny knew exactly what he was doing."

"You mean Scrawny saved the old redwood because he knew it would one day provide a secret entrance for SCNAC?" Miriam was intrigued.

"It wouldn't surprise me," Libra replied.

• • •

They drove past the western gate to the campus, continuing along Empire Grade for several miles through dense redwood forest.

"We're using the back entrance to avoid all the security checks," Miriam told them. "No offense, Commander, but there's no way those security officers would allow a cat into the facility."

"None taken, Dr. Steinberg. I'd have the same trouble getting you or Adele into a Gatosian nonlinear accelerator facility."

Miriam pulled off Empire Grade onto an unnamed dirt road. She stopped in front of a chain gate, got out and unlocked it, and drove for another quarter of a mile on the narrow twisting lane bordered by madrone and ceanothus. The road was poorly maintained and they pitched up and down like a rowboat on a stormy sea.

"I guess the university wants to discourage any visitors," Adele observed."

"It's practically impassable in the winter during the rainy season," Miriam remarked.

At length they arrived at a small cleared area and Miriam parked the car.

"We go the rest of the way on foot," she said.

Miriam led them along a narrow winding path that plunged into a dense stand of redwoods. Adele and Libra noted that the trees were arranged in rings around huge, decomposing stumps, vestiges of that old primeval forest that Melissa Sprowell and old Scrawny had sought to preserve, if only symbolically, by saving one of the ancient colossi. By now the stump sprouts were themselves monumental giants, although mere neophytes compared to their parent trunks. Parts of the path were blocked by fallen trees, which posed more of a problem for Miriam and Adele than for Libra, who easily walked under them. After some time they came to the base of the enormous old redwood

tree whose girth far exceeded the others, indicating its natural affinity with the generation of stumps rather than
with their sprouts.

"This is it. This is Scrawny's tree," Miriam said, patting one of the many huge burls that bosomed out of the
imposing base. "And here's the crevice that Melissa
Sprowell and Scrawny used to enter the hollow of the tree."

Adele and Libra gazed at the narrow opening in the
huge hollow trunk, which seemed to part like petrified curtains, inviting them to enter its darkened interior. Libra
had never seen such a majestic life form. Nothing on Gatos
even approached it in magnitude or awe-inspiring beauty.
Her eyes followed the massive trunk upward, a soaring
splendor of arching branches and delicate green lacework.
Adele, too, was moved by the tree's magnificence.

"I can see why Scrawny wanted to save this tree," said
Libra.

"Yes, it's breathtaking," echoed Adele.

"Let's go inside," said Miriam.

Adele and Libra watched as Miriam slithered through
the crevice and disappeared. They did the same, and were
immediately plunged into darkness. As their eyes adjusted, they could see Miriam take hold of what appeared to be
a small outgrowth or burl on the interior wall. She pushed
upward and an entire section of the wall moved with it,
exposing a panel of blinking lights. After punching in a
pass code, Miriam placed her hand flat against a small
video screen.

"This checks out my fingerprints," she confided.

Finally, she spoke her last name softly into a microphone and a synthetic voice said, "Entry approved. Please
stand against the wall before activating the elevator."

"Stand as far back as you can," she said. "I'm going to
raise the elevator."

Miriam pushed the green button and a circle of
ground in the middle of the tree suddenly slid aside and an

elevator composed of white metal and clear plastic rose like a bubble to the surface. "We call the elevator the 'White Rabbit,'" said Miriam, smiling. The door opened and Miriam walked in, followed by Libra and Adele.

"This is amazing," said Adele. "I had no idea this was here."

"Although the facility is pretty well hidden, we're in the process of tightening security even more," Miriam confided.

"Have there been any problems?" Adele inquired.

"We're not sure yet, but according to the FBI, some of our data may have fallen into the hands of a foreign power. We're trying to determine the source of the leaked information. We may be dealing with a mole."

Libra was surprised to hear that a mole would trouble itself with such matters. On Gatos moles were usually shy and retiring creatures and rather harmless. Perhaps it had merely overheard something it shouldn't have, since the facility was located underground, and had passed the information on to a friend quite innocently?

"Commander, I should probably carry you," said Miriam, scooping Libra up into her arms before she had time to protest.

The elevator descended swiftly and smoothly down a smooth metallic shaft extending through the soil horizons beneath Scrawny's tree and was soon penetrating solid limestone well beyond the reach of the tree's deepest roots. Moments later the shaft abruptly opened out and they saw that they were at the center of a brilliantly illuminated open space resembling a vast underground warehouse.

Libra squinted.

"My, it's bright in here," Adele remarked, shielding her eyes.

The White Rabbit gently halted, the door slid open, and Miriam and Adele stepped out onto the smooth composition floor. Huge steel cylinders looped around overhead like gigantic floating pretzels and then tunneled off through the limestone in myriad directions. Whole sections of the peripheral walls were lined with video screens, computer terminals and a seemingly endless array of switches and blinking, multicolored lights monitored by a dozen or so technicians in white lab coats. Most wore their lab coats unbuttoned, and Libra could see that their attire underneath was very informal. Most wore jeans or shorts and running shoes. Scattered about the facility were small open areas with vending machines labeled "SCNAC Bars." Here, small groups of employees were seated on white resin patio chairs around tables, sipping coffee and partaking of Danishes, donuts, and other goodies. A burst of laughter issued from one such gathering near the elevator.

"What do you think of the lab so far, Commander?" Miriam asked.

"It reminds me of an early prototype nonlinear accelerator built in my great-grandmother's day," Libra replied judiciously. "Modern ones are much more compact. But I think this one will do fine for our purposes—with some modifications, of course."

Suddenly Libra did a double-take. Out of the corner of her eye she thought she detected a familiar face. She leaned over Miriam's shoulder and scanned a cluster of tables arranged around some vending machines. Her gaze focused on a rather thin woman with shoulder-length, wavy blond hair seated at a table drinking coffee from a plastic cup. She was wearing a white lab coat like all the other technicians. The coat was unbuttoned, revealing a long black sweater, and tights. Libra imagined her face framed by different hair styles, and suddenly it came to her. It was Finessa Debbitz! She was wearing a blonde wig. Evidently Rolf Trammel was using one his own company officials to spy on SCNAC. As Libra stared at Ms. Debbitz, the disguised chief accountant suddenly looked up and caught a glimpse of Libra's face above Miriam's right shoulder. Libra ducked, but it was too late. She had been spotted. When she peeked over Miriam's shoulder again a moment later, Ms. Debbitz was gone.

"We'd better go straight to Howard's office," said Miriam, "before anyone inquires about Libra."

They quickly strode across the facility to the corner where Dr. Ng's office was located. Miriam knocked on the door. After a brief pause, the door opened and a smiling bespectacled man with a round face and thinning gray hair greeted them.

"Miriam, how nice to see you!" Dr. Ng eyed Libra, and was about to raise an objection to Miriam when he spotted Adele. "Adele Cameron, what a pleasant surprise! Come in. Have a seat."

Miriam and Adele entered the office and sat down in the soft leather chairs facing the broad desk in the center of the room. Libra sat in Miriam's lap facing the desk. Looking about, she saw that the walls were papered with data: graphs, charts, cloud chamber photographs of particle collisions, the wispy trails of subparticles exploding like tiny fireworks. A large whiteboard was covered with equations. Libra noticed that Dr. Ng's computer was a Cameron, not a Dogma.

"You know, we don't allow animals in the facility, Miriam," he said. "If you and I don't follow the rules it sets a bad example for the staff." And turning to Adele, " Sorry, Adele, I didn't mean to begin on a negative note. It's a matter of protocol."

Libra bristled at Dr. Ng's reference to her as an "animal." It took every ounce of her self-control to regain her equanimity.

"I understand, Howard" Adele replied. "But please don't blame Miriam. She's only trying to help me."

"Help you?" Dr. Ng repeated, puzzled.

Miriam and Adele looked at each other. Finally, Miriam spoke.

"Howard, we have something truly remarkable to tell you, so prepare yourself."

Howard Ng eased back in his chair and brought his fingers together, as if to brace himself. A well-organized, disciplined man, he was wary of surprises.

"I'm listening," he said slowly.

"It concerns this cat," Miriam continued.

Dr. Ng cast his gaze on Libra. Libra was relieved that the director had not patronized her by patting her on her head or scratching her under her chin. That almost made up for referring to her as an "animal."

"Howard, I'd like you to meet Commander Libra Shimagrimicka, space explorer from the planet Gatos!"

On cue, Libra stood up in Miriam's lap, leaned over the desk and extended her right paw.

"I'm very pleased to meet you, Dr. Ng," she said.

Dr. Ng gasped.

Chapter 24
Screechium at SCNAC

ONCE PROFESSOR NG HAD RECOVERED from the shock of being spoken to by a cat and was formally introduced to Libra, he became quite excited and shook Libra's paw over and over, until she defensively withdrew it.

"I'm delighted and honored to meet you, Commander. Please excuse my earlier remarks. It isn't every day we have the privilege of entertaining an ambassador from another solar system. I would be more than happy to assist you in any way possible. Now what can we do for you?" Dr. Ng asked.

Once again Libra carefully reviewed the events leading to Voca's damaging her chip, which had resulted in her being stranded on Earth. For the sake of brevity, she omitted most of her other encounters, asking Dr. Ng's understanding in view of the urgency of the situation. Dr. Ng was most cooperative and did not pursue such obvious questions as how she had come to meet Adele and Miriam. "I'm bursting with curiosity about your adventures on Earth, Commander," he said, "but Adele can fill me in about them later. I'm particularly excited about helping you to make screechium. If we succeed, it would be Earth's first metallic anti-matter element."

"It shouldn't take too long," said Libra. "We only need a tiny amount. But I'll have to reconfigure your accelerator."

"I'm placing SCNAC entirely at your disposal, Commander," said Dr. Ng. "The screechium experiment is as of this moment our highest priority." Reaching into a drawer in his desk, he drew out a set of blueprints and spread them on the desk before Libra. "Here's the current layout of the accelerator," he said.

While Libra studied the blueprints, Dr. Ng summoned his chief engineers and theoretical physicists on the intercom, and, as soon as they had assembled in his office, quietly explained the situation to them. At first they thought Dr. Ng was playing a practical joke and they burst out laughing, but quickly sobered as Libra climbed up on a stool in front of the white board and, using a blue marker pen, made a quick but accurate sketch of the current layout of the accelerator.

"Thank you for your attention," she said politely. "This is the present configuration of your nonlinear accelerator. Now here's how it needs to be modified. . . ."

Needless to say, everyone in the room that afternoon was awestruck by Libra's mastery of unified field theory, black holes, white holes, quantum gravity, mew-ons, quasi-matter, yarn theory, and branched space-time, although much of what she said went so far over their heads that it sounded like complete nonsense. Nevertheless, they scribbled furiously in their notebooks, hoping to make sense of it later. However, they were frustrated at being unable to fully comprehend the theoretical underpinnings of Libra's requested modifications to the accelerator, even though they were perfectly capable of implementing the changes that needed to be made.

As soon as Libra was satisfied that Dr. Ng and the engineers understood what needed to be done, she terminated her lecture abruptly. When the engineers continued to pepper her with questions, Adele intervened.

"I'm sure the Commander would love to answer all your questions," she said, "but she's already told us far more than Gatosian Space Commission regulations permit. Besides, the situation is exceedingly urgent. There's no time to waste!"

With a sigh, the engineers and physicists put away their pens, and rose from their seats.

"Let's get started immediately," Dr. Ng said, rising from his chair and leading them out of his office.

After some initial confusion, the overhaul of SCNAC went quickly and well. Donning a lab coat and construction hat provided by Dr. Ng, Libra began barking out orders (metaphorically speaking) to the engineers and technicians, while marching from one sector of the facility to another at a pace that left Howard Ng, Miriam, and Adele gasping for breath.

News of the screechium experiment spread like wildfire through the facility, and soon the entire staff was pitching in. Within hours they were ready to test the new accelerator configuration, and everyone held their breath as Libra peered at the results as displayed on the monitor. After checking and rechecking the data, she turned and addressed the assembled crowd.

"Ready for production," she pronounced calmly, and all the scientists, engineers, and workers of SCNAC, including Dr. Ng, cheered at the good news. Two hours later, they had generated a tiny amount of screechium, all that was needed to manufacture Voca's new nanochip, and had placed it in a suitable magnetic containment field—the core of a powerful portable electromagnet—for transport to the U. C. Santa Cruz satellite facility at Mountain View. The more stable quasi-matter was placed in a small vial which Adele dropped into her purse for safe keeping. Bottles of champagne, which the scientists at SCNAC had stored away in refrigerators for just such an occasion, were brought out and popped open, and Dr. Ng led a gracious toast to Libra, amidst cheers, laughter, and high-fives.

As they were about to ascend the White Rabbit to Scrawny's tree, Libra turned to thank Dr. Ng, while Adele and Miriam looked on.

"I'm in your debt, Dr. Ng. When I give my report to the Gatosian Academy of Sciences, you can be sure that I won't forget your generosity. . . ."

"It has been a privilege to assist you, Commander," replied Howard Ng. "We at SCNAC are grateful to you for giving us this glimpse into the future of particle physics."

"There's one last thing I need to tell you. . . ."

"Yes, Commander?"

"I think I've identified your 'mole,' the spy who's been stealing your secrets. . . ."

Adele and Miriam were flabbergasted when Libra announced that she had identified the spy who'd been stealing data from SCNAC—none other than Finessa Debbitz, the chief accountant at Dogma Computers! They talked about it excitedly during the drive over Highway 17.

"Of course I can't prove that she's been stealing data," said Libra, "but if she had nothing to hide, why was she wearing that blonde wig?"

"And to think," Miriam exclaimed, "we thought her name was 'Doris Schultz', and had her working in the data management department . . ."

"—where she was perfectly positioned to purloin classified files and documents from SCNAC," added Adele.

"Howard said he was calling in the FBI," said Miriam. "They should be able to get some answers."

While they were talking, Miriam looked into the rearview mirror and noticed with alarm that they were being followed by four motorcyclists. Just past the summit, the four motorcyclists drew even with them and scowled at them threateningly. They were bearded and wore tattered black leather vests over their grimy T-shirts. Their long hair flapped wildly in the wind beneath shiny black helmets. The roar from the four chrome-laden Harleys, all of which lacked mufflers, was deafening. Smiling malevolently, the lead driver drew his right forefinger across his throat and then pointed straight at each of them in turn. But just then a police car pulled onto the highway, and the four motorcyclists quickly dropped back. The next time Miriam looked in the rear view mirror they were nowhere in sight.

"Whew!" said Miriam. "I'm glad they're gone. That was pretty intimidating!"

"Those are members of the Marauders gang, I'm sure," Adele replied.

Fortunately, no further incidents of that sort occurred during the rest of the drive to the Mountain View campus. Adele called ahead to Derek Lampley at Feynman Laboratories to let him know they were on their way.

It was evening when they arrived in the large parking lot in front of the Molecular Engineering Building. Derek Lampley was there to greet them, along with his colleagues, Lucille Gavin and Violet Takahashi. The latter were sitting in one of the campus's electric shuttle cars, a modified golf cart for transporting important visitors and dignitaries directly from their cars to the door of their building.

"Adele, good to see you!" said Derek. A tall, thin man with a thick mane of grayish hair, gold-rimmed spectacles, and a British accent, he had been a long-time collaborator and close friend of both Felix and Adele Cameron.

"Hi Derek! Hi Violet and Lucille!" Adele returned. "Do you all know Miriam Steinberg from SCNAC?"

"From reputation, of course!" Derek replied. "I'm happy to meet you in person, Miriam!"

"Derek, Violet, Lucille—I'd like you all to meet Commander Libra Shimagrimicka from the planet Gatos," said Miriam. Since Adele had previously prepared Derek, Violet and Lucille by calling ahead, to Libra's great relief they merely shook her paw.

"Welcome to Mountain View, Commander. It's an honor to meet you," each of them said in turn.

"Likewise, I'm charmed," said Libra, always pleased to have an opportunity to use another one of her Earthling idiomatic expressions.

"We'll take the shuttle car," smiled Violet.

"I have the Feynmanator all warmed up and ready to go," said Lucille. "I presume you have the screechium, Commander?"

"It's in the trunk," said Libra.

Adele popped the lid to the trunk and Miriam lifted the small wooden box by the handle and gave it to Derek.

"It's contained in a magnetic field," she said. "Antimatter. Don't drop it . . . or kablooey!"

Derek blanched. "I'll try to remember that," he replied.

Violet Takahashi guided the shuttle directly to the side door of the laboratory, where they disembarked and swiftly entered the building.

"Remember which room it's in?" Derek asked Adele.

"The one to the right at the end of the hall?"

"Right. You remembered!" Derek teased.

"How could I forget the scene of all those parties we used to have."

"Those were heady days, eh Adele? Printing the first nanocircuits. . . ."

"Heady, indeed!" said Adele. "But I think today is going to take the prize for headiness!"

"Adele," Libra interrupted, "if I could borrow your cell phone?"

"Why yes, of course," said Adele. She reached into her purse and handed the phone to Libra.

"Lucille," said Libra, "I need to modify the frequency

of this cell phone so I can download the schematics of the antimatter-furry logic-power interface nanochip from Voca, my colleague and on-board computer, to the Feynmanator. I'll need some tools."

"Certainly, Commander, the shop is next door," said Lucille Gavin, and the two of them went into the next room.

"Another thing, Lucille—"

"Yes, Commander?"

"You'll have to use a magnetic-field stylus, not a regular stylus, on the Feynmanator."

"Or else kablooey, right?"

"Right," said Libra.

Meanwhile, Adele, Derek and Violet prepared the quasi-matter matrix according to the recipe Libra had written out for Adele during a brief lull in the activity at SCNAC. Among other features, the matrix exhibited the remarkable facility of preventing matter–anti-matter interactions, thus stabilizing the whole structure. Having prepared the matrix, they filled the magnetic stylus with screechium; it was much like filling an old-fashioned fountain pen with ink, although, of course, far more dangerous.

Fifteen minutes later, Libra and Lucille returned with the modified cell phone to the main laboratory, where the others had gathered expectantly around the Feynmanator. It was about 10:00 PM.

"Okay," said Libra, "I'm going to call Voca. As soon as I've made contact with her, I'll download the specifications to the Feynmanator. . . ."

Chapter 25
The Return of
the Marauders

AT PRECISELY 10:17 PM, Chopper Alpha from the Dogma compound at Altaperro thundered low over the Santa Cruz Mountains, followed closely by Choppers Beta and Gamma. Jug Maraud, attired in military camouflage, rode shotgun in the lead copter, his feet propped against the control panel. The gold chain of Libra's communicator hung out of his right shirt pocket. Just twelve minutes earlier, they had received a brief transmission that, although encrypted, had allowed the technicians at Dogma to determine the exact coordinates of the source of the transmission. Voca's location now showed up as a red circle on the screen of the onboard computer, while the helicopter's position was indicated by a blue circle. They were still a few miles away. Maraud leaned out of the open side of the chopper and scanned the rocks and brush of the terrain beneath him with wide-angle infrared binoculars. As his eyes probed the ruby glow of the receding landscape he kept listening for another of those strange-sounding signals from the communicator. On the ground below, Frank Carne and the Marauders were rapidly approaching the base of the mountain on their motorcycles. Maraud flipped the switch of the radio.

"Maraud to Carne."

"Yeah, I'm here. . . . *Que pasa?*" Carne spoke into the receiver inside his motorcycle helmet.

"No sign of 'em yet," answered Maraud. "Where are youse?"

"Should be there in ten minutes," Carne shouted into the receiver.

"Okay. Don't blow it."

"Don't worry," Carne snarled. "By the time we're through with this mountaintop there won't be a blade of grass left standin'. We'll find 'em."

"Dat's what youse said the last time, and youse got snookered by a pussy cat!"

"Hey, now look, Jug, that's unfair. . . ."

"Maraud out."

Jug Maraud clicked off the receiver and sucked on his cigarette, turning the tip a bright orange. The smoke oozed out his nostrils. Wrinkling his brow he again lifted the binoculars to his eyes. Then he gazed at the screen. The blue circle was inching closer to the red circle.

"We're almost there!" he said to the pilot.

Down below, still crudely concealed beneath piles of brush, Voca sat stoically, her power reduced to the bare minimum needed for life support in order to avoid discovery. Inside the cabin, Hank and Pinny trembled in each other's arms. They could hear the merciless thumping of the vast whirling blades of the choppers closing in on them from above. Despite her recent training in Katari, Pinny again felt like a tiny, helpless Earthling cat, and all the fight drained out of her.

"Oh, Hank! I'm so scared. I thought I was brave and smart like the Commander, but now I see I'm just a silly little coward after all," she said.

"Hush, Pinny, you're no coward. Remember, you're

just a junior cadet. Your training is incomplete. If the Commander were here, she'd know what to do. Maybe Voca can think of something. . . ."

"I can think of lots of things, Hank," answered Voca, "but all of them require power and mobility. I don't dare try to contact the Commander again because it would only serve as a beacon. I fear my transmission of the schematics for the anti-matter nanochip may have already given away our location. The best we can hope for now is that the Commander will return with my new nanochip before the Marauders find us. Otherwise, we may never get back to Gatos." At the thought of her commander's plight, Voca's circuitry suddenly overflowed with remorse. "Oh dear, oh my!" she choked. "And all because of my sneeze!"

"Don't feel bad, Voca, it's not your fault," Hank purred soothingly, patting her gently on the console. "You'll see. Everything's going to be all right."

"I wish I had your confidence," said Voca, "but I'm afraid things are looking bad right now. In fact, the time has come for you and Pinny to save yourselves before it's too late. The Commander and I will always be grateful to you whatever happens. But you must leave, now. Don't worry about me. There's nothing more you can do."

"We won't abandon you, Voca," said Pinny staunchly. "Remember the Nineteenth Article of Space Academy Regulations: 'the ship's safety is paramount.'"

"I know," Voca replied gently. "But it wasn't meant to apply to you."

Despite the terrifying nearness of the enemy, Hank felt a strange sense of calm, as if the spirit he had beheld in the forest clearing—the golden lioness—were still with him. He closed his eyes and sat quietly for a moment in deep concentration. Finally he spoke.

"Pinny, I'm going outside. If I can get their attention, maybe I can draw them off the way I did before."

"No, Hank," Pinny cried out in alarm. "It's much more dangerous this time. I can feel it in my bones!"

"There's no other way," said Hank. "If we don't do anything, they're bound to find us. It's only a matter of time. Voca, do you have any other communicators?"

"In the right-hand drawer next to the Commander's stasis chamber," said Voca. "But you can't use it. It would draw them to us."

Hank reached into the drawer, pulled out one of the small, black devices and held it in his paws.

"Hank," cautioned Voca, "I don't advise . . ."

"Maraud will use any transmission we make to track us, right?" Hank said as he tied the communicator around his neck.

"Yes, but . . ."

Hank interrupted. ". . . So I'll make a dash for it to the other side of the mountain, and when I get there I'll turn on the communicator. That'll divert their attention for a while. And by the time they figure out they've been tricked the Commander will have returned with the chip."

"Hank, it's much too risky!" cried Pinny, holding on to her brother tightly, and burying her face in his thick fluffy coat. "What if they track you?"

Hank gently disengaged himself from her grasp. "Pinny," he said firmly, "after I leave, run back down the mountain to the house and see if Cathy, Adele, and the Commander have returned. Explain everything to them. Tell them Voca is in great danger!"

Hank pressed the button by the door and the small metallic panel hissed open. He paused at the threshold and then turned around to face Pinny once again, his brow furrowed with concern. But as he gazed upon his sister now, his features relaxed to a smile, and the white blaze of his chest seemed to shine with an unearthly brilliance against the abyss of the night.

"Remember, Pinny, whatever happens," he said

tenderly, "be brave!"

"Hank, don't go! " Pinny pleaded.

But it was too late. Hank had already disappeared into the darkness.

Frank Carne's Harley was the first to tear into the meadow grass, followed by a thundering armada of Marauders. The helicopters continued to circle the area like vultures scanning for a carcass. The tremendous noise hurt Hank's eardrums as he dashed down the ramp. As soon as his paws touched the ground he crouched down flat against the cool earth and tried to get his bearings. He could hear the beating of his heart even over the din of the helicopters and motorcycles, which encircled them in an ever-tightening noose. With a start he realized that his plan would not work. The Marauders were much too close. Through the tangle of branches and leaves he could see about fifty of them a mere hundred paces away, sending up huge sprays of dirt and filling the air with their war hoops and battle cries. In their hands were metal pipes that they used to beat the brush, leaving a torn and flattened land-scape in their wake. Any minute now one of them might veer off from the pack and discover Voca's hiding place. Hank swallowed hard. There was not enough time to deliver the communicator to the other side of the mountaintop. There was only one thing to do. With a powerful leap he tore through the branches and scrambled out into the meadow, hugging the ground as closely as possible. There were a few remaining untrampled areas and he navigated through them, using the weeds for cover. As soon as he judged he was far enough away from Voca's hiding place, he stopped, turned on the communicator, and took off like a shot.

Jug Maraud had just tossed his cigarette butt out the door of Chopper Alpha when he heard a steady beeping noise coming from his right shirt pocket. At first he looked around for its source, until he realized it was coming from the communicator.

"We got a signal!" he exclaimed. He reached for the microphone. "Chopper Beta, Chopper Gamma. We got contact! Follow us!"

"I'll put it on the screen," said the pilot.

The red circle was flashing, and as it flashed it moved rapidly toward another sector on the grid.

"It's moving!" cried Maraud.

"It may be some type of vehicle," said the pilot. "Let's fly down and get a closer look."

Maraud screamed into the microphone.

"Maraud to Carne! Come in, Frank!"

"Got some excitement?" responded Carne laconically after a pause.

"Sector J-17! Moving fast! Get on it! I'll give you some light."

"Hot dog! Party time! Carne out!"

"It won't be long now!" Maraud shouted, shaking his fist at the meadowland below.

Directly below, Hank was galloping faster than he'd ever run before, faster than he imagined it was possible to go. He had only one thought in mind: to reach the safety of the forest with its ground cover of poison oak. As he lunged toward the woods the weeds lashed at his face and the night air keened like a banshee past his ears. His mouth was slightly ajar to gulp in more breath and his tongue felt cold and dry. He was surprised that the horrendous din of the helicopters and the motorcycles seemed to abate, and all he could hear was his own labored breathing and the frenzied pounding of his paws on the damp earth. As if in a dream he saw the headlights of the motorcycles alter their courses and then close ranks behind him.

At a command from Maraud, all three helicopters trained their halogen floodlights on sector J-17, illuminating the ground below in large glaucous circles. Hank squinted in the unnatural brightness, but forced himself to keep his eyes open so that he could maintain his pace without stumbling. The wind from the whirling blades gusted down upon him, flattening the weeds, eliminating whatever meager cover the meadow still provided. Completely exposed, he had no choice now but to run until he reached the sanctuary of the woods, or until he could run no more.

"There he is!" shouted Carne on the lead cycle. "It's that gray and white cat again! He's got something around his neck. Let's get 'im, boys!"

The Marauders gunned their engines and let out a terrifying battle cry as they fanned out behind their leader. Frank Carne was thirsting for revenge for the scalp lacerations Hank had inflicted on him and for the humiliating and miserable episode of the poison oak. He would get that cat if it was the last thing he did! Drawing his pistol, he took aim and fired.

The bullet pinged against a rock to Hank's right and Hank instinctively altered his course to the left. However, this direction led him away from the forest, so he darted back to his right again.

"He's heading for the woods!" screamed Maraud over the radio in Carne's helmet.

"Don't worry. We'll cut 'im off!" Carne yelled. He stood up on his cycle and waived his right arm from side to side over his head. "Spread out and circle around," he shouted. "If that cat reaches the woods you're dead meat!"

Two more shots rang out, raising small clouds of dust, one to Hank's left and one to his right. Each time he flinched, but stayed on course. At the periphery of his vision he caught a glimpse of the Marauders gaining ground on his flanks. Soon they would close in and encircle him in a lethal trap. The forest was still over a hundred and fifty meters away. If he could only make it. If only he had wings and could fly! If only he could shrink himself to the size of a mouse and scurry down some gopher hole deep in the ground! If only he could make himself invisible so the Marauders would roll right past him and never know he was there!

"He's entered sector J-18!" shouted Maraud.

But Carne was no longer answering. He was in full pursuit, his eyes wide open, his veins bulging in his neck and temples, his mouth locked in a continuous battle cry. Shot after shot he fired at the elusive quarry until he had used up all his rounds. Cursing, he flung the useless pistol onto the ground and bore down even faster.

Less than one hundred meters now separated Hank from the sanctuary of the woods. He could see the ragged selvage of the forest before him and smell the fragrance of the leaves and the pungent odor of damp logs. Every muscle in his body was aflame with exhaustion as he drove himself onward. And with each excruciating leap, Frank Carne, a thick steel pipe upraised in his right hand, gained ground on him from behind, and the two lines of Marauders on either side approached each other in front of him, closing the circle. Looking up, he saw that one small gap yet remained in the ever-tightening noose through which he might slip if only he were fast enough. Summoning all his strength, Hank surged forward with such acceleration that Maraud, watching from overhead, screamed into the microphone: "Watch out! He's gonna make it!"

But this time Hank was not to reach the forest. The circle closed in front of him just as he was about to burst through, and he had to veer sharply to the left to avoid being crushed by the spiky wheels. The Marauders erupted in a mocking cheer as Hank darted desperately around inside the circle seeking an opening, but they had closed ranks, leaving no avenue for escape. Carne sat atop his bike in the center of the circle, watching Hank's futile dash with grim satisfaction.

"We got 'im!" he barked into the hidden microphone in his helmet.

"Finish him off, and get his communicator," ordered Maraud. "Then head back to sector J-17. We still haven't found his base of operation."

"Check," Carne answered.

After twice dashing around inside the grinning circle of Marauders and finding not even a sliver of an opening through which to escape, Hank gave up and came to a halt. Trembling with fatigue, he lay down on his stomach in the grass and tried to catch his breath. As he drew in the cool night air in deep drafts, he gazed up at Carne, who was looking down at him with hatred in his eyes.

Carne got off his bike and started to approach Hank holding the pipe down by his right side.

"So, you thought you could mess with Frank Carne and get away with it, eh, pussy cat?"

As he spoke, Carne slapped the steel pipe ominously against the open palm of his left hand.

"Mash 'im good, Frank!" one of the Marauders shouted out. "Remember the poison oak!"

"Yeah, I've still got an itch that I need to scratch real bad, and you're that itch, pussy cat!" sneered Carne.

Carne raised the pipe over his head and charged swiftly at Hank's prone figure. Grunting, he swung the pipe down with savage force, but Hank leaped aside and the pipe struck dirt.

Hank's agility surprised even himself. From somewhere deep within his consciousness a spark had been struck, and that spark kindled instantly into a small flickering flame as he looked up at Carne unafraid. The image of the mountain lion came back to him now, and he felt the powerful presence of his forebears, the ancient ones who roamed these meadows free and unmolested long before the humans came. With arched back and fur bristling, Hank emitted a deep growl that startled Carne as he stalked his trapped prey.

"So the pussy cat's become a lion, has he?" Carne scoffed, but there was a note of tension in his voice.

Suddenly Carne lunged forward onto his knees and wielded the pipe like a baseball bat, swinging sideways in an attempt to knock Hank off his feet. But to Hank's heightened feline vision, Carne seemed to be moving in slow motion, and he was easily able to anticipate the blow. Well before Carne managed to swing the pipe around, Hank was in his face, and with claws extended he took a swipe at Carne's left cheek. The claws contacted the face near the left ear, hooked into the soft flesh, and dragged sharply all the way to the nose, leaving a bright red swath in their path. Blood instantly welled up from the torn flesh and poured down Carne's cheek.

"Aiiiiiiiiii! My face!" he cried out in pain.

"You idiot!" Maraud, who had been watching it all from the chopper overhead, shouted into his helmet. "You numbskull!"

"Give me a gun! Give me a gun! I'm gonna kill that damn cat!" Carne swore at his comrades, trying to stanch the flow of blood with his bandanna.

The Marauders, who had only temporarily been shocked into silence by Carne's cry of pain, revved up their bikes and tried to close in on Hank, but the circle was tight and they were too close together. Jammed against each other, legs scraped against tires, and some of the bikers were forced to drop back, creating small but penetrable gaps in their formation. Hank saw his opportunity. He waited until the Marauders were practically on top of him, and then suddenly made a dash for it, zigging and zagging between wheels until he reached the outer perimeter of the circle and broke free.

The edge of the forest was now only fifty meters away. Hank plunged ahead with the last bit of strength he possessed. Carne was right behind him and closing in fast.

Hank heard the report of the gun as the force of the bullet knocked him off his feet, and he rolled over and over.

"I got 'im boss!" Frank Carne yelled jubilantly into the head phone of his helmet. "I shot that gray and white cat! He's a goner!"

"It's about time!" replied Jug Maraud. "I'm heading back to Altaperro. There's been a break-in at Fangri-La and the boss needs me. Continue searching sector J-17 for their hide-out. Choppers Beta and Gamma will stay on to help. Over and out."

But Hank, the fur of his right flank soaked in blood, struggled back to his feet and limped on toward the forest's edge. It was just a few more meters!

"The cat got up, boss! He's gonna make it into the woods again!" shouted one of Carne's men.

"Over my dead body, he will!" snarled Frank Carne, as he lurched forward on his motorcycle. "Over my dead body!"

Carne charged ahead with his front tire rearing up like a stallion. At the forest's edge, Hank glanced up and saw the raised front wheel of Carne's bike directly overhead, bearing down on him like a buzz saw. And then there was a confusion of wheels and branches and chrome and dirt and black leather and fur and leaves, as the motorcycle plunged headlong into the forest and disappeared in the darkness.

Chapter 26
Voca Rises

IT WAS ABOUT 10:45 PM when Adele, Libra and Miriam pulled into the driveway at the Cameron house in Los Gatos. Although Libra had displayed some exasperation with the "primitive Earthling equipment," in the end they had succeeded in constructing Earth's first superconducting-furry logic-antimatter-power interface nanochip with screechium quantum gravity switches in a quasi-matter matrix— a routine bit of manufacturing in Gatos to be sure, but a marvel of computer engineering on Earth. Now, with her task at last completed, Libra (wearing her safety belt this time) sat smugly on the front seat between Miriam and Adele, holding the newly minted nanochip in a plastic sandwich bag securely on her lap.

During the drive back from Mountain View, Libra decided it was time to reveal Cathy and Carlos's plan to infiltrate Altaperro. She explained that the object of the plan was to recover Felix Cameron's lost notebook and to obtain evidence that would prove that Trammel was behind his death.

Adele was naturally sick with worry when she heard the news. She was particularly distressed that Libra hadn't told her earlier.

"I wish you had said something to me about it, Commander," Adele cried angrily. "I might have been able to talk her out of it."

"I'm sorry, Adele," Libra responded apologetically. "Cathy swore me to secrecy. I was opposed to her taking such a risk, but she insisted."

"Cathy is strong-willed, Adele," Miriam pointed out. "I doubt you could have stopped her even if you had known about the plan ahead of time."

Adele suddenly wept, and reached into her purse for a Kleenex.

"I suppose you're right, Miriam," she said, dabbing the tears from her eyes. "Commander, I apologize for snapping at you. It's not your fault, I know. I've been under a lot of stress lately, and I'm just worried about my daughter. . . ."

Libra put her right paw on Adele's hand.

"I promise you, Adele, as soon as I get Voca airborne, I'm going to pay Rolf Trammel a visit at Altaperro and make sure that Cathy and Carlos are safe," she said firmly.

"I would be most grateful if you would, Commander," Adele replied. "I have no one else to turn to."

Miriam turned the wheels sharply into the driveway and pulled to an abrupt stop in front of the garage. The car doors were thrown open, and the three companions bounded out of the vehicle. Libra, a step ahead of Adele and Miriam, pushed back the front gate and trotted briskly up the path, holding the sandwich bag containing the nanochip in her left paw.

The front door was ajar.

"My word!" Miriam gasped, gazing into the living room.

Libra stood in front of her, staring in disbelief. The living room was in a total shambles. Furniture had been overturned; pictures ripped off the walls, their glass panes smashed and thrown onto the floor; the rug had been slashed and torn; and the kitchen and dining room floors were littered with shards of broken glass and china. A chill ran down Adele's back, and she shuddered. Libra was simply aghast. Of all the qualities of human beings she had observed during her brief sojourn on Earth, the one that made the profoundest impression was their seemingly limitless capacity to carry out the most incomprehensible mischief. She made a mental note to discuss this puzzling evolutionary quirk at length in her report to the Gatosian Academy of Sciences.

The three of them went from room to room surveying the damage. It seemed that whoever had broken in wasn't simply looking for something; they had been intent on destruction. Pottery and vases had been smashed against the wall, and the computers in the bedrooms had been crushed and battered. Cathy's room, in particular, had been devastated, as if the intruders had been in a rage. Since Adele had gone pale and looked unsteady on her feet, Miriam gave her a comforting hug. Even Libra, with all her training and discipline, was taken aback by the mayhem. Clearly it was meant to serve as a warning.

Adele had seen enough. They walked out the front door and conferred on the porch.

"This is the work of the Marauders. I'm sure of it!" Libra declared. "They must have come here right after they quit following us back on Highway 17."

"I'd better call the police immediately," said Adele.

"You can use my cell phone," said Miriam. "The line from the house has been cut."

Just then, Pinny rounded the corner of the house at a full gallop and came skidding to a halt before them. Her fur was standing on end and her sides were heaving. She was extremely agitated.

"Commander! Commander! Something terrible has happened!" Pinny cried out in Gatosian.

"What is it, Pinny?"

"The Marauders have surrounded Voca! They've got helicopters with big searchlights! You've got to come immediately!"

"Where's Hank?" Libra asked.

"He's trying to lure them away with a communicator," cried Pinny. "His plan was to run to the other side of the mountain and then turn it on to attract their attention. Oh, Commander, I'm so frightened!"

"What's going on?" asked Adele. Pinny's urgent report in Gatosian had sounded like just so much mewing to her, although she could tell from their expressions that the news was not good.

"The Marauders have returned to the meadow," Libra explained in English. "They've got helicopter back-up this time. It sounds serious. They're closing in on Voca. I've got to get back immediately and install the new nanochip. It's time for Voca to fly!"

"I'll go with you!" said Adele.

"So will I!" Miriam declared.

"Shouldn't you call the police first and report the damage to your house?" Libra queried.

"Later," said Adele. "Hurry! There's no time to lose!"

Okay," replied Libra. "Pinny and I will take the short cut over the back fence."

"It'll take us a little longer," said Adele. "We'll have to take a bike path that leads up the mountain. We'll meet you in the meadow!"

"Look for the pile of redwood boughs near the path," Libra called out.

Without further ado, Libra and Pinny ran to the back yard, hopped over the fence, and were soon racing up the trail toward the meadow. It was pitch black and they had no flashlights to guide them. This was not much of a hindrance to Pinny with her excellent night vision, but Libra kept tripping on stones and stumbling on the tree roots that extended across the trail here and there.

They soon reached the edge of the meadow. In the distance they could hear the roar of motorcycles punctuated by the deafening clatter of helicopter blades beating the air. Thanks to Hank's efforts, the focus of the action was a considerable distance away from the ship, and they were able to make their way to Voca's hiding place unobserved.

They reached the pile of redwood boughs, crawled through the foliage, dashed up the ramp, and entered Voca's cabin. Voca greeted them emotionally.

"Commander!" she cried. "I'm so glad to see you!" The relief in her voice was palpable.

"Calm yourself, Voca my dear," said Libra. "I have the new nanochip. Soon you'll be airborne. Pinny, hand me the screwdriver from the drawer underneath the console!"

Pinny dashed to the console and handed Libra the small screwdriver. A moment later and Libra had removed the panel from the wall.

"Forceps!" Libra requested, holding out her paw. "They're in the same drawer, Pinny."

Pinny retrieved the micro-forceps and slapped it into Libra's waiting paw. Opening up the sandwich bag, Libra carefully inserted the delicate forceps and fished out the tiny chip. Next she reached into the exposed circuitry behind the panel door and, with a flick of her wrist, deftly inserted the nanochip in its proper location.

"I'll just spot-weld it in," she said, reaching for the small toolbox underneath her seat by the console. Donning a pair of magnifying lenses, she reached in with her micro-welding tool and in no time the chip was anchored into place.

"Done!" she said. She stood up and looked out the door.

Miriam and Adele had just arrived and were calling from outside the pile of redwood boughs.

"Pinny, I'm going out to talk to Adele and Miriam. Ready Voca for take-off."

"Aye, Commander," said Pinny crisply. Although she was still worried about Hank, she derived comfort and confidence from following the Commander's orders and applying her newly learned Gatosian Space Academy protocols.

"Miriam, welcome to Voca's hangar," Libra quipped. "If we had more time I'd introduce you formally, but that will have to wait."

"Is there anything we can do to help, Commander?" Adele asked.

"Yes—if you would remove the branches covering Voca, it would prevent their scattering around and hitting someone when we take off."

"We'll take care of that. Commander," Miriam volunteered.

"Adele, before we go to Altaperro, Pinny and I are going to make a sweep over the meadow and put the Marauders out of commission. Once we've got the situation under control, you and Miriam must try to find Hank. He risked his life to save Voca."

"Of course, Commander," said Adele.

"Good-bye, then," Libra said. "We'll see you when we return from Altaperro."

"Good bye, Commander!" called Adele and Miriam, as they quickly removed the branches from Voca, exposing the small craft to the open sky for the first time since the night she had landed.

Libra and Pinny took their seats before the console, Pinny acting as co-pilot. The ramp retracted and the door slid shut.

"Begin the count-down," Libra ordered Pinny.

Pinny pressed the green button marked "GO" (in Gatosian, of course) and Voca began counting down:

"Ten—nine—eight—seven—six—five—four—three—two—one—*lift-off!*"

Like a thunder clap, her powerful engines blasted on, and Voca lifted off!

Back on the ground, Adele and Miriam watched in awe as the diminutive space ship levitated quickly into the sky. Miriam turned to Adele:

"Well, if I still harbored any doubts about Libra's identity when we came up here, watching Voca's take-off was the clincher!"

Pinny was pressed against her seat by the force of Voca's vertical lift. She had never experienced anything quite like it. Libra noticed Pinny's surprise.

"It's always a thrill the first time," she smiled. "Okay Pinny, now what do you see approaching us off the port bow?"

"A couple of helicopters, Commander, and one of them is starting to shoot at us."

"All right, Pinny, now you're going to get a chance to practice your sharpshooting skills," said Libra. "I want you to disable those helicopters by knocking out their rear rotors."

"Aye, Commander!"

Pinny aimed one of the anti-matter cannons at Chopper Beta's rear rotor, and pushed the firing button.

"Direct hit!" cried Libra. "Good shot, Pinny!"

Its steering mechanism damaged, Chopper Beta started spinning helplessly out of control, forcing the pilot to make an emergency landing on the field below. Chopper Gamma, however, rose up level with them and commenced firing upon them with a machine gun. The bullets bounced harmlessly off Voca's impenetrable hull.

"It's my turn now," said Libra, taking aim with the antimatter cannon.

Seconds later the rear propeller of Chopper Gamma exploded, and the rudderless craft, after hesitating for a moment, began spiraling out of control, landing with a great "whump!" on the meadow very close to Chopper Beta.

"Nice shot, yourself, Commander!" Pinny exclaimed.

"Now we're going to do a little crowd control before we go check up on Cathy and Carlos at Altaperro. We'll give these Marauders the best night's sleep they've had since they were babies."

Voca made a sudden turn and dropped swiftly on a curving flight path toward the downed helicopters, like a hawk pursuing a mouse. The two pilots ran in terror.

"Stand by to administer the de-animator ray, Pinny."

"Aye, Captain," said Pinny.

"Now!" shouted Libra.

As Pinny pushed the button, a beam of cobalt blue light emanated from the front of the ship. The ray completely enveloped the fleeing pilots, who immediately slumped to the ground. Voca again swept back up to a higher altitude, staying as invisible as possible.

"They aren't dead, are they?" asked Pinny.

"Of course not," Libra reassured her. "They're just sleeping very soundly. The de-animator ray is based on the same technology as the stasis chambers. It's just a little more powerful. As long as the exposure is brief, it's perfectly harmless."

"Let's put them all to sleep," said Pinny. "Then they can't hurt Hank!"

"That's the plan," Libra replied. "Voca, please do an infrared scan and display the locations of all the motorcyclists on the screen."

"There they are—by the edge of the forest," cried Pinny.

"They're bunched together," said Libra. "Perfect. This will make things easier. Hang on! We're going to sing these bikers a lullaby they can't resist."

Voca swooped down from the sky for a second pass, this time heading straight for the Marauders on their motorcycles. The Marauders had just watched Frank Carne plunge into the forest after Hank. The next moment they had heard a couple of loud crashes behind them, and when they turned around they saw the two choppers falling out of the sky like wounded insects.

"Choppers Beta and Gamma were shot down," yelled Hog Spline, as he pulled nervously at his red beard. "Did anyone see what the hell happened?"

The other gang members all shook their heads.

"Hey, what's that comin' our way?" asked another gang member, a young man wearing a bandanna on his head and a patch over one eye. "Looks like a big Frisbee with headlights!"

"That ain't no Frisbee," said another. "Looks like a flyin' saucer!"

"You're crazy!" shouted Hog Spline. "You been watchin' too many TV shows."

"Whatever it is, it's too close for comfort. I'm gettin' out of here!" yelled the other Marauder, frantically trying to back his bike out of the tight formation.

But it was too late. They were trapped in the circle by the weight of their own bikes. Before any of them could get away, Pinny blasted them with the de-animator ray, and they all fell asleep instantly. One by one they keeled over, along with their motorcycles, like a line of dominoes collapsing in a circle onto the welcoming grass. Without constant gunning, the engines of the toppled motorcycles soon stalled, and as they sputtered out, one by one, the quiet of the meadow was restored. Except, of course, for the snoring of the Marauders.

Libra brought Voca out of the dive and they rapidly gained altitude.

"You seem to have quite a talent for this, Pinny!" Libra remarked. "That should hold the Marauders till morning at least. Now, it's off to Altaperro! I promised Adele I'd check in on Cathy and Carlos. Hang on! Voca will take us there in one jump!"

"Here we go!" cried Voca, darting skyward.

Chapter 27
Pinny Earns her Stripes

CARLOS GLANCED OVER AT CATHY and saw a look of fierce determination on her face. Far from being cowed by the sudden appearance of Trammel and Maraud, she almost seemed to welcome the confrontation. It was quite a change from the timid and insecure girl he'd first met over a year ago.

Jug Maraud kept his pistol trained on Cathy and Carlos, while Rolf Trammel walked with studied slowness over to the large curving window with its sweeping view of Silicon Valley, now glittering with lights in the darkness. As he gazed down over the Valley, Trammel seemed lost in thought. Finally he spoke.

"You are a stupid, insolent girl," he said. "You and your mother should have taken my advice and sold Cameron Computers to me a long time ago." Turning from the window, he sat down behind the large mahogany desk, placing his pistol before him. "Now you're going to die. Didn't you ever hear the story of how curiosity killed the cat?" He smiled wanly. Cathy thought he looked tired and worn out, perhaps because of being awakened in the middle of the night, although she thought she detected a kind of weariness that even sleep cannot cure.

"At least I found out what happened to my father," Cathy replied. "You and the Marauders murdered him!"

"Yes, but you'll take that knowledge to the grave." Trammel responded coldly. "You and your cowboy detective friend here."

"Don't be so sure, Trammel," said Carlos. "Do you think we'd be stupid enough to come here without back-up?"

"And what sort of back-up might that be?" Rolf Trammel asked disdainfully. "The police have given me a clean bill of health. The mayor and I are bosom buddies. Altaperro is private property, and you've just been caught trespassing. Whatever evidence you found would be thrown out of court! Looks like the law is completely on my side, right Jug?"

"Right, boss," repeated Jug Maraud.

Maraud walked over to Carlos, waving his pistol in his face.

"Me and youse have a little score ta settle," he said, and then suddenly punched Carlos in the stomach so hard it made him double over.

"Tsk, tsk," Trammel clicked his tongue in mock disapproval. "Jug, please! No violence! The dogs will take care of our guests! And after they get through with them, we'll hand over whatever's left to the authorities."

"Just one question, Trammel," said Carlos, struggling to catch his breath. "I know all about your shady business practices in the computer industry. I know about your illegal dumping of toxic waste. And I know about the contracts you put out on my brother and Dr. Cameron. But I'm curious about one thing: how did you happen to get involved in a spying operation at SCNAC?"

"I thought the great cowboy detective would have figured it all out by now!" Rolf Trammel replied. "Okay, I'm rather proud of our foray into espionage, so I'll grant you your last wish before you become dog food. You see, despite the excellent quality of our computers and the great esteem with which we are held in the industry, lately we've been having a slight cash-flow problem. You may have read that SCNAC has developed a prototype machine for producing an anti-nuclear ray. They say it will be used to decontaminate nuclear waste dumps. But what you may not know is that the government is also planning to use this technology to neutralize the radioactive stockpiles of certain foreign governments and terrorist organizations. For obvious reasons, these governments and terrorist groups would love to get their hands on the plans for the anti-nuclear device."

"And I'll bet they're willing to pay big bucks for the information," Carlos added.

"You bet your booties, Cowboy!" Trammel crowed.

"Which must come in handy, since Dogma Computers has been losing money hand over fist," said Cathy.

Trammel glared at Cathy.

"And how has your pathetic little company been doing lately, Miss Cameron? Not very well, I understand. Despite all the palaver about innovation and technical superiority, Cameron Computers is about to go under. Yes, I admit it— I'm a businessman, not a scientist. I've never taken much interest in technology, myself. I believe in making money. It's the American way!"

"You're not a businessman, Trammel. You're a parasite and a murderer," Cathy shot back defiantly.

"Shut your mouth, girlie!" Jug Maraud answered, advancing menacingly with his pistol raised.

"Back off, Maraud!" returned Carlos. Cathy had never seen Carlos so angry before.

"Never mind, Jug!" Trammel intervened, with a look of pious suffering on his face. "I think we've observed the amenities long enough. It's getting late. Gnash and Gnaw haven't eaten all day! They must be ravenous by now. Tie these trespassers' hands behind their backs, Jug, and we'll pay a little visit to the kennels. I can see the headlines now: 'Ex-Vegas Sheriff and Girlfriend Killed by Guard Dogs During Burglary Attempt!'"

Maraud guffawed so strenuously that he began to choke.

"Hear that, Valdez? That's your obituary!" he said.

While Jug Maraud was tying Carlos's hands together, Cathy glared at Rolf Trammel, debating whether or not to attempt an escape. In the background, she could see the lights of Silicon Valley shining in the distance far below, and the stars glimmering in the night sky above. It was as if the Valley itself were a pool of water reflecting the light of the stars. Then strangely, one of the stars began to move toward them and momentarily a curious blinking object hovered into sight just outside the window. It was about the size of a picnic table and had the shape of an inverted milk bowl. Cathy recognized it at once.

"Voca!" she cried out before she could prevent herself.

"What?" Trammel shouted in irritation. "Don't try any—"

But before Rolf Trammel could finish his sentence, the window shattered behind him, knocking him to the floor and showering him with glass shards, as Voca flew into the office, her multi-colored lights flashing. Slowly and majestically she landed on the carpet next to Trammel's desk, while Jug Maraud merely gaped in stunned silence. Carlos, seizing the opportunity, whirled around and kicked Maraud's gun out of his hand. The gun flew onto the floor and slid underneath the couch against the far wall.

The door to the ship hissed open, and Libra and Pinny quickly dropped onto the carpet. Cathy was startled to see Pinny walking on her hind legs behind Libra as they strode down the ramp. She looked quite smart in one of Libra's uniforms—though it was a trifle too large for her.

"Boss, it's the black cat!" exclaimed Maraud, on his

knees frantically groping for his gun under the couch.

"Commander!" cried Cathy, rushing up to her. "I'm so glad to see you!"

"Better untie Carlos," Libra said. "We'll deal with Maraud and Trammel. Pinny, here's your opportunity to show off your new Katari moves."

Trammel, who was still dazed by Voca's violent entry, had just risen to his feet, and was gingerly pulling fragments of glass out of his toupee.

"Hiiiiiii *yahhhhh!*" shouted Pinny with surprising ferocity for a small tabby, and gave Rolf Trammel such a solid whack on the shin with her right front paw that he immediately dropped to the floor in pain, rocking back and forth while cradling the bruised member in his hands. Pinny wasted no time, pummeling his stomach and back until he pleaded for mercy. As the final *coup de grâce,* she bit him on the hand, which was a bit of pure improvisation and not part of her Katari training.

Meanwhile, Libra strode up to Jug Maraud, who was still straining to reach his pistol. Tapping him on the shoulder, she grasped his left wrist with both paws and twisted his arm behind him until he yelped. She then threw him over her shoulder with a flourish, and finished him off with a Baton Twirl. When he was finally deposited on the floor, Jug Maraud was dizzy and confused. Carlos and Cathy then dragged the two defeated and disconsolate scoundrels to the center of the room and Carlos tied their hands behind their backs.

"Nice work, Commander. The game's over for you, Trammel!" said Carlos.

Rolf Trammel glared at Carlos with fury in his eyes.

"You'll never get out of here alive, Valdez! You're in the belly of the beast. This is my domain. There are twenty-five security guards and pit bulls patrolling the grounds. Your freedom is short-lived!"

But even as he spoke, the wail of an approaching

siren could be heard in the distance. Cathy rushed to the side window.

"It's the sheriff's department!" she exclaimed.

Cathy noted with pure satisfaction the expressions of shock, horror, and dejection that passed in rapid succession over the faces of Rolf Trammel and Jug Maraud. Rolf Trammel's defiance of a moment ago seemed to melt away as he slumped on the floor.

"Cathy," said Libra. "It looks like things are pretty well under control here. Pinny and I are going back to the meadow to look for Hank. He was defending Voca from the Marauders."

"Okay, Commander," answered Cathy. "Carlos and I will be there as soon as we can."

"Better bring some deputies with you. There are a bunch of Marauders sleeping on the meadow, and they'll be needing a roof over their heads—a prison roof!"

Without further ado, Libra and Pinny ran up the ramp and quickly prepared Voca for take-off. With a roar of her engine, Voca lifted off the carpet and flew out the window, just as the sheriff and several of his men burst into the room.

"What was that?" one of the deputies asked, glancing at the burn marks on the carpet.

"What was what?" Carlos asked innocently. "I didn't see anything."

"It was a black cat and a vicious tabby in a flying saucer!" shouted Trammel, wild-eyed. The deputies stared at him incredulously. "Officers! Am I ever glad to see you!" he went on. "We caught these two intruders burglarizing my office. They then carried out a vicious assault on our persons, handcuffed us as you see, and were making off with valuable and highly private documents when you fortunately arrived in the nick of time. As a law-abiding citizen and a personal friend of the mayor's, I demand that you arrest them immediately and unlock these handcuffs!"

A tall, athletic-looking man stepped forward. "Not so fast, Mr. Trammel," he said. "I'm Sheriff Nasi Mandela. We're here to serve you with a warrant to search the premises. Mr. Valdez, if you've taken anything from Mr. Trammel's files, please hand it over right now."

Carlos pulled out his wallet and opened it, showing a silver badge. He also took a small folded-up piece of paper from his back pocket. Sheriff Mandela looked closely at the badge and document.

"Hmmm . . . FBI, all right . . . and a letter from Supreme Court Justice Rondale approving the break-in for national security reasons. I guess that trumps me, Agent Valdez. Weren't you with the Las Vegas Sheriff's Department? I thought you quit after your brother was shot?"

"That was just a ruse to throw Trammel and his people off the trail," said Carlos. "I've been working under cover for the Bureau since then."

Cathy gave Carlos a look of surprise, and Carlos smiled back and shrugged.

"I'll be happy to hand over the documents," Carlos said to Sheriff Mandela, "as long as you're willing to share them with our people."

"Of course," Sheriff Mandela replied.

"Just one question," Carlos asked. "How did you get the warrant?"

Just then Howard Ng stepped forward from the back of the crowd of deputies.

"Howard!" Cathy cried out. "What are you doing here?"

"Hi Cathy!" Dr. Ng said. "I'm so glad to see you're all right! Agent Valdez, I think I can answer your question. You can thank a mutual friend of ours (I think you can guess who) for the information that led to the warrant. She recognized one of our employees at SCNAC—someone we knew as 'Doris Schultz'—as Rolf Trammel's chief financial officer, Finessa Debbitz. We contacted the Bureau and they told us about your undercover operation. They also ran a more thorough check on Doris Schulz and found that all her credentials and references had been faked. We were able to establish that Ms. Debbitz, *a. k. a.* Doris Schultz, had opportunities to steal or copy all of the stolen data. The FBI informed the sheriff, and they got the warrant."

Carlos laughed. "Well, I guess we're in Libra's debt on all fronts. Too bad we can't convince our 'mututal friend' to hang around. The criminal element wouldn't stand a chance!"

"Howard," said Cathy, "can you drive us to our car? We've got to get back to my house."

"Be glad to, Cathy," Dr. Ng replied.

"Sheriff Mandela, I think you'll find the Marauders gang sleeping in a meadow in the hills behind my house. Can some of your deputies follow us?"

"You seem to have all the answers tonight. Sure, I'll dispatch some of my people to accompany you."

Without hesitating a moment longer, Cathy, Carlos, Howard, and several deputies left the Altaperro building, jumped into their cars and headed toward the meadow where Voca had landed.

Chapter 28
A Difficult Farewell

MOMENTS AFTER DEPARTING FROM ALTAPERRO in the Diablo foothills, Libra, Pinny, and Voca arrived at the meadow in the Santa Cruz Mountains. Streams of fog drifted in through the passes from the coast, and here and there ragged strands of mist hovered over the grass, but otherwise it was a beautifully clear night, brightly illuminated by a waxing moon. Using Voca's sensitive sonar system, they quickly located Adele and Miriam near the spot where Hank had entered the forest just ahead of Frank Carne. As they flew nearer, they could see the beams of their flashlights. Off to the side, the Marauders still lay snoring in the moonlight beside their collapsed motorcycles. Pinny brought Voca in for a perfect landing directly in front of Adele and Miriam.

"How's Cathy?" Adele asked the moment Libra disembarked.

"She's fine, Adele," Libra reassured her. "The sheriff arrived with a warrant, and Carlos handed over all the incriminating files. Turns out Carlos has been working for the FBI all along, monitoring Trammel's activities. Trammel, Maraud, and the rest of their crew will be cooling their heels in prison for quite some time. Any sign of Hank?"

"No," said Miriam. "We've been searching ever since you left, but we haven't been able to find him anywhere."

Libra thought for a moment. "Pinny, didn't you say he was wearing one of Voca's communicators?"

Pinny confirmed that he had.

"Then Voca should be able to locate him," said Libra. "Wait, I'll be right back."

Libra ran back into the ship. A moment later she returned.

"Voca's found him! He's in the woods directly north of here!"

They entered the woods at the same point where Frank Carne had attempted to crush Hank with the front wheel of his motorcycle. By moonlight alone they were able to discern that the grasses, ferns and lupines growing at the border of the forest were torn up and ground into the earth at the point where the huge motorcycle had plowed its way through. A few meters further, Adele's flashlight picked up a shiny metallic object. They had come upon the bent and twisted remains of a Harley wedged between two redwood trees.

"One of the Marauders' motorcycles," said Adele, peering at the wreckage.

"Any sign of the Marauder who was riding it?" asked Libra.

"No," replied Adele. "No sign of the rider."

"Looks like something has been dragged this way," Miriam motioned them toward the interior of the forest. "And there's blood."

Adele, Libra, and Pinny followed Miriam as she tracked the marks through the forest litter.

"It's leading to a clearing just ahead," she announced.

At the edge of the clearing they discovered a crumpled human form lying face down in the duff.

"Who's that?" cried Miriam, rushing forward.

Miriam and Pinny held the flashlights while Libra and Adele turned the man over. Blood covered his throat and his shirt was soaked with it.

"It's Frank Carne, the leader of the Marauders," Libra said solemnly. "He's dead."

"Looks like his neck is broken," said Adele. "But how could he have come this far from his motorcycle with a broken neck? It doesn't make sense!"

"What are those wounds in his throat," Miriam asked.

Libra examined them closely.

"Those are the bite marks of a large cat," she exclaimed. "It's remarkable! I didn't know you had any big cats around here."

"We used to have mountain lions," said Adele. "But there are very few left. In fact, I didn't know there were *any* in these parts."

Miriam knelt on the ground beside Frank Carne's body and examined the forest floor with her flashlight. Near his head was a patch of dirt where the leaf litter had been scraped away.

"Look at these paw prints," she said. "They're huge!"

Even Libra was impressed.

"It certainly looks like mountain lion prints," said Adele.

"Commander, Look!" Pinny suddenly exclaimed, pointing toward a large flat redwood stump at the center of the clearing. Adele and Miriam trained their flashlights on the stump, but all they could see was a swirl of mist reflecting the light back into their eyes.

"Do you see it, Commander?" Pinny asked in breathless awe.

"Yes, Pinny, I see it." Libra replied, and she stepped forward, seized with a deep sense of wonder and longing. As she did so, the fog thinned momentarily, and she beheld with almost unbearable clarity the luminous vision of a huge mountain lion standing in the middle of the altar-like surface. But even as she glimpsed it, it melted again into the fog and dappled darkness. Libra cried out something in Gatosian—which even Pinny couldn't understand.

"Did you see anything?" Miriam asked.

"No," Adele replied hesitantly, "I don't think so." But Libra said nothing.

"There's Hank!" Pinny cried. "On the stump!"

Again, Adele and Miriam directed their beams to the flat mossy surface, illuminating Hank, sprawled out limply on his side. Pinny ran and jumped up beside him.

"Hank! Hank! What happened to you?" cried Pinny, tears streaming down her face. She could see the small hole in his side where the bullet had entered, although his fur seemed to have been cleaned of blood.

At first Hank did not respond. Then his eyes fluttered open and he saw Pinny who was crouched by his side clasping his right front paw in both of hers.

"Pinny," he whispered hoarsely. "Did we save Voca?"

"Yes, Hank, we saved Voca!" Pinny exclaimed, fighting back her tears.

"Is . . . the . . . Commander . . . safe?" he asked. He was gasping for breath and his sides heaved.

"Yes, Hank, I'm fine," said Libra. "Hank, you were very brave. You lured the Marauders away from Voca and saved her life. When I return to Gatos, I'm going to recommend you for the Royal Order of the Paw, Gatos's highest honor."

"Gatos's . . . highest . . . honor . . ." Hank repeated. And then his breathing grew more labored and he closed his eyes.

"Hank! Hank! Don't leave me!" cried Pinny.

But Hank could no longer hear her. He was not really there. He was sitting on his favorite rock in the meadow with his eyes half closed, smelling the sweet spring wildflowers and listening to the sounds of crickets and birds. The sun was setting on the horizon and the entire mountaintop was ablaze in golds and greens and purples. Soon he would get up and head back home, where Cathy would be waiting for him with a bowl of nice warm milk and . . .

"Pinny—?" he called out, and his breathing ceased.

Pinny began to sob uncontrollably. Adele and Miriam stood over them silently as Libra took Hank's pulse and examined his eyes. She sighed heavily.

"I'm afraid he's gone," she murmured, placing her arm around Pinny.

"Don't die, Hank!" Pinny wailed, shaking his inert shoulders. "Please don't die!"

Libra choked back her own tears as she held Pinny in her arms and rocked her back and forth. Suddenly she stopped short and jumped to her feet.

"Pinny, there's one last hope," she said. "Adele, carry Hank's body out to the ship. We'll put him in one of the stasis chambers! There's not a second to lose! Come, Pinny! Let's get the chamber ready!"

While Libra and Pinny ran ahead, Adele scooped Hank's body up in her arms and ran with him back to the meadow, Miriam running along beside her. They reached Voca's door and Adele extended her arms and handed Hank to Libra and Pinny, who quickly carried him to a small drawer similar to the one in which Libra had slept during her journey to Earth. They arranged him in a comfortable position on the pillow and then Libra pushed the button that caused the drawer to retract into the cabinet. Even before the clear lid clamped shut, Pinny could see him bathed in the cool blue light of the stasis chamber.

"Will it bring him back to life, Commander?" she asked hopefully.

"No, Pinny, not as far as I know," Libra said. "But it will prevent any further deterioration. And by the time we return to Gatos another hundred years will have passed. By that time Gatosian medical science may have advanced greatly. Perhaps they will be able to do something. At least we can hope."

"Then Hank would become a Gatosian," said Pinny. "He'd like that!" And then she began to weep once more.

Just then Cathy and Carlos arrived breathless beside the ship.

"We got here as soon as we could," said Cathy. "We found the notebook in Trammel's files. Sheriff Mandela is letting us keep it for now," she exclaimed, handing the precious document over to her mother. No one spoke. She looked anxiously from face to face.

"How's Hank?" she asked next.

Libra broke the news to her, and Cathy, too, burst into tears. Instinctively, she picked up Pinny, who had come out to meet her, and cradled her in her arms. Pinny put her paws around Cathy's neck and the two of them wept silently together.

The hour was getting late, and the fog had entirely drifted away. Off in the distance they could see the sheriff's deputies attempting to arrest the pilots of the downed helicopters, who were unable to stay awake long enough to have their rights read to them. Soon they would be moving on to the Marauders lying in a circle along with their motorcycles—and they would discover Voca. Libra decided that now was a propitious time for her to depart for Gatos. Pinny hopped to the ground, and she and Libra embraced for a long time. Pinny was distraught.

"Don't be sad, Pinny," Libra said comfortingly.

"I can't help it," Pinny answered. "With Hank gone, I'll have no one to talk to in Gatosian. And with Voca gone, there will be no one to teach me English."

"You'll have other Earthling cats. . . ." Libra noted.

"But I'm not like Earthling cats any more. I'm different. I've changed. Besides, I could never have the opportunities on Earth that I could on Gatos."

"You're right, Pinny. I won't deny that." Libra looked out across the moonlit meadow. "You know," she continued, "you're welcome to come with me back to Gatos if you want to."

Pinny hesitated before answering. "Thank you, Commander," she said, "but I couldn't. Cathy needs me too much. Hank and I have been her pets ever since she was a little girl. And now that Hank is gone, I'm all she has left."

"I understand your feelings," said Libra, smiling sadly at her little Earthling protégé.

"Thank you for everything, Commander," she said. "I'll never forget you!"

Then Pinny stepped back, and Cathy, Adele and Miriam knelt down on the grass to give Libra a hug as well.

"Thanks for helping me to get back to Gatos," she told them. "Without you, I never would have been able to replace the damaged nanochip. Also, give my thanks to Howard Ng and Derek Lampley, and everyone at SCNAC and the Feynmanator Lab."

"We will, Commander. We will," said Adele and Miriam, with lumps in their throats. "Thanks to you, the reign of Dogma has ended."

Finally, Libra shook hands with Carlos.

"I'm sorry we never had time for you to teach me the Baton Twirl," he smiled.

"Pinny can teach you!" Libra replied.

"Will we ever meet again?" asked Carlos.

"Not unless Gatosian scientists have come up with new breakthroughs in my absence. The journey takes a hundred years. But anything is possible!"

"You've made me believe it!" said Carlos.

And then it was time for Libra to take her leave. Slowly she walked over to the ship and slowly, almost reluctantly, she climbed the ramp. At the entrance, which gave off a yellowish glow in the darkness, she turned to wave good-bye to her Earthling friends for the last time. Pinny, who had climbed up on Cathy's shoulder to get a better view, was becoming more and more agitated. She was torn between her fervent wish to go with Libra and Hank, and her loyalty to Cathy. She had made her choice, but was it the right one?

Glancing down, Pinny saw that Carlos had put his arm around Cathy's waist, and that Cathy was leaning against his shoulder. And she realized that Cathy was no longer a little girl. Perhaps Cathy didn't really need her so much any more. . . .

Suddenly Pinny leapt down from Cathy's shoulder and dashed up the ramp to Libra's side.

"Commander!" she cried out in Gatosian. "I'm going with you!"

"Lieutenant Pincushion, welcome aboard!" smiled Libra.

Libra entered the ship while Pinny stood for a moment, waving good-bye to her startled humans. Then she, too, disappeared into the ship. The ramp retracted, and the door slid shut.

Then the four humans stood back a safe distance as Voca lifted slowly off the ground. In the clear night sky, they were able to follow Voca's trajectory for quite some time, and through the circular window they could see the diminishing figures of Libra and Pinny waving.

"She wanted to go," said Cathy, fighting back her tears as she waved good-bye to her dear little pet.

"Yes," replied Carlos. "It was the right choice."

Dawn was breaking over the tops of the redwoods. A diffuse light was already beginning to filter in from the east, and overhead the sky was turning blue throughout the Valley. Ineluctably, the sun crept above the horizon, shining on the Diablo Range, gilding the twin towers of Fangri-La; shining on the rooftops and streets of Silicon Valley, reflecting off windows and the wings of gulls; and shining on the peaks of the Santa Cruz Mountains, on the outstretched boughs of redwoods, and on the lush green meadows with their palettes of wildflowers.

Cathy, Carlos, Adele, and Miriam stood transfixed in the gathering morning, until Voca's lights finally winked out like a star. Then slowly and thoughtfully they began the long walk down the familiar trail.

Epilogue

THE EVIDENCE UNCOVERED *by Cathy Cameron and Carlos Valdez helped convict Rolf Trammel, Jug Maruad, Finessa Debbitz and a host of other Dogma officials and members of the Marauders motorcycle gang of crimes ranging from homicide to espionage, and everything in between. Trammel and his top cronies all received life sentences and were sent off to spend the rest of their days in the strongest, strictest, and most secure prisons in all of California. Altaperro was converted to a state park, and the hated Fangri-La was dismantled, to the considerable relief of the citizens of San Jose. Gnash and Gnaw are undergoing rehabilitation at a clinic for abused animals, and have shown great improvement in their temperaments, although they are still not considered ready for adoption.*

With the creative genius of Silicon Valley no longer stifled by Dogma, a renaissance in computer engineering was ushered in. Among the bright new companies that emerged like spring wildflowers after a conflagration was Libra Computers, formerly known as Cameron Computers. Adele Cameron was able to apply the breakthrough in superconductivity documented in her husband's notebook to greatly enhance the speed of conventional computers. The hot new Libra Computer was an instant success, and its worldwide popularity contributed greatly to the economic recovery and well-being of the Valley. Three bronze statues in front of the Libra Computer Building honor the three brave cats who made it all possible: Libra, Hank, and Pinny.

It should certainly come as no surprise that Cathy and Carlos were married the year following Libra's departure. Even while helping her mother run Libra Computers, Cathy—after graduating magna cum laude *in computer engineering at U. C. Santa Cruz—went on to obtain her doctorate in bioinformatics at the same institution, where she won plaudits for her conceptual design of the first DNA-based bio-organic computer. Eventually she applied this design to the construction of the first intelligent computer, for which she received the coveted Turing Prize. Carlos named the new computer "Vocita."*

As for Libra, Pinny, Hank and Voca—they're still traveling across the Milky Way galaxy, hopping from branch to branch of space-time, homeward bound.

Appendix
Song Lyrics

1. Libra Shimagrimicka
(Prologue)
Amanda, Beatrice, and Mark Shelby, Johnny Freeman
Amsea Group, copyright 2002

You were asleep for a hundred years,
As you journeyed through space and time.
When you left your world there were tears,
So your eyes blurred the three moons.
The night was light not bright as day,
And the band played your patriotic tunes.

You've landed and awakened in our world,
In the dim light of one full moon.

Chorus
Commander Libra
Shim-a-grim-ee-ka
You cat from another world.
Your planet of Gatos,
Sounds like our town of Los Gatos.
You're sleek and black.
Commander Libra Shimagrimicka,
Oh, why must you go back!

You met Henry, our domestic cat
When you wandered down from the hill.
But he was much too scared to chat.
He jumped in the air and screeched,
Hairs on his back standing on end,
He dashed away so he couldn't be reached.

You've landed and awakened in our world,
Your likeness just took off for home.

Chorus

"Earthling! Wait! Come back! I won't attack,"
You yelled at our stupid feline.
Maybe tomorrow he'll come back.
You'll give him another try.
The humor of it makes you laugh.
The jolt to your heart nearly made you die.

You've landed and
Awakened in our world.
See the light of another day.

Chorus

2. The Landing
(Chapter 1)
Amanda, Beatrice, and Mark Shelby
Amsea Group, copyright 2002

Earth's a blue marble suspended in space.
It emits signals all over the place,
Uploads everything to the Internet.
Voca the computer has downloaded all she could get.
She's used up her hard drive and most of her DRAMs.
Now comes the cache and the balance of her RAMs.

Chorus
Turn on, turn on, it's time for the landing!
Turn on, turn on, it's time for the landing!

Voca wakes up, getting ready to land,
Plays "Green Again" by the Gatosian band.
Downshifts from thrusters to quantum paw drive
Onto evanescence, then down to nimblynimbly five.
She says, "Uh, oh, we're tumbling end-over-end!
Better wake the Commander to make a mend."

Chorus (repeats)

"I must wake Libra in the stasis chamber,
Make her aware of our extreme danger."
As the light goes from blue to lavender,
Libra awakes from her hundred-year slumber.

Chorus (repeats to fade)

3. Ah-Choo, Voca
(Chapter 2)
Amanda, Beatrice, and Mark Shelby, Johnny Freeman
Amsea Group, copyright 2002

Chorus
Ah-choo!
Ah-choo, Ah-choo, Voca!
Furry logic mental mocha.
Your heart's all rarin' to go.
This is in slow mo.
Ah-choo, ah-choo, Voca!
Lay down, now, don't provoka.
Better stay at home now.
You need a dose of warm ozone.

"Ah-choo!"
"Bless you!"
"Thank you very much."
"Please try not to sneeze, Voca my dear.
It's not good for your circuits."
"Okay, Commander.
Commander?" "Yes, Voca my dear?"
"I think I'm going . . . to sneeze."

Chorus

"There, between the anti-viral program and the nanodox,
You should be feeling ship-shape in a few hours."
"Thank you, Commander Shimagrimika,
I'm feeling much better already."
"It's too late to take off right now.
So, while you're resting,
I'm going to take one last walk around the sun."
"Okay, Commander, but be careful."

Poor Voca, he had to go and catch 520 viruses from the Internet.
Oh, boy!

Chorus (repeats to fade)

4. Sunshiny Day
(Chapter 5)
Amanda, Beatrice, and Mark Shelby, Johnny Freeman
Amsea Group, copyright 2002

Chorus
Oh what a sunshiny day.
I have to get away.
Oh what a sunshiny day.
I wish that I could stay.
I brought you something good to eat.
It's tuna sushami.
A Gatos delicacy—felines' favorite treat!

I've slept for a hundred years.
I've conquered all my fears.
It's time to see what this world has to give.
I'll hide my ship somewhere.
I'll pass away my cares,
And go explore. See how these people live.

Chorus

What's that beneath that plank?
Looks like a cat named Hank.
I'll get him out with a tasty treat.
It's tuna sushami.
I'm not your enemy.
I thought we'd get a chance to meet.

Chorus

Its scent is so good.
Its taste is divine.
How can we resist with all this sunshine?

Chorus (repeats)

5. Making New Friends
(Chapter 6)
Amanda, Beatrice, and Mark Shelby, Johnny Freeman
Amsea Group, copyright 2002

Here kitty, kitty.
Someone's calling you, Hank.
She's kinda pretty and she knows you by name,
With brilliant eyes and a smile so bright.
You'll introduce me when the moment is right.

Chorus
Making new friends, like silver and gold.
More people to know.
Making new friends, like silver and gold.
A place I can go.

It's nice to meet such a friendly face.
My name is Libra; I'm from outer space.
Tell me please; can you help with my ship?
All I need is a microchip.

Chorus (repeats)

6. Venturing Forth
(Chapter 7)
Amanda, Beatrice, and Mark Shelby, Johnny Freeman
Amsea Group, copyright 2002

Venturing forth. See the world.

[Can you decipher this conversation?]

Venturing forth. See the world.

[Is Libra about to compromise her orders?]

Venturing forth. See the world.

[Who is the worrywart?]

Venturing forth. See the world.

The first hundred people to decipher the spoken words and correctly answer the three questions will receive a little present from Libra.

7. Whose Secrets AreYou Stealing Now?
(Chapter 8)
Amanda, Beatrice, and Mark Shelby, Johnny Freeman
Amsea Group, copyright 2002

All the computers are breaking down.
Screens going black without sound,
Interrupting school, work and play.
Dogma without a word to say.
I can't take this, wanta break it.
These things are a waste of space.
Now I see what Dogma's up to.
Stealing secrets to save some face.

Chorus
Whose secrets are you stealing now?
What will you do when the word gets out?
Stockholders have a right to know.
What you're up to.

All the employees are at home, now.
The buildings's empty. No one's around.
Gotta find evidence somehow.
Open the files. Don't make a sound.
Gotta find out what they're up to.
There must be a trace somewhere.
In the desk drawer there must be more,
Evidence to support our case.

Chorus (repeats)

Yeah, yeah
Whoa yeah, whoa yeah
Whoa yeah, who-o-o-o-oh
Whoa yeah, whoa yeah
Who-o-o-oh, who-o-o-o-oh

8. Hank's Discovery
(Chapter 8)
Amanda, Beatrice, and Mark Shelby, Johnny Freeman
Amsea Group, copyright 2002

Across the meadow
Is where I'll find your ship.
Up on the hill,
Could be an airstrip.
I know it's somewhere,
Beneath the redwood bows.

Chorus
Little Earth cat, talk to me, talk to me.
I found a Gatosian tongue from history.
"Meeoww, brrow brrrrrrrow,
Meeeee-ow, weeeee-ow, brrrrrrrow," said Hank
"Let mee-ee out!"

Don't be scared.
I'll be a friend to you.
Let's have a talk.
You'll learn a thing or two,
About our language.
Maybe you'll learn it soon.
Now listen closely,
So you won't get confused.

Chorus

Here's a peace offering,
To help to break the ice,
A little broiled salmon,
Filet with Gatos spice.
Don't be shy.
Go on and have a ball.
I know that you want it,
And the taste is outta sight.

Chorus

9. Destination Dogma
(Chapter 9)
Amanda, Mark, and Beatrice Shelby
Amsea Group, copyright 2002

Chorus
I'm on my way to Dogma
In a return-for-repair hardware box
My destination's Dogma
I'm cushioned by Styrofoam rocks
I'm on my way to Dogma
I need to make a computer chip
My destination's Dogma
This is a necessary trip

10. Libra Learns the Truth
(Chapter 10)
Amanda, Beatrice, and Mark Shelby, Johnnyn Freeman
Amsea Group, copyright 2002

The meeting started with a feeding frenzy . . .
Dogma's president says,
"We've got to stop new ideas from enemies . . .
Too bad about Cameron's crash."
He says with a malevolent grin,
"We'll do what it takes to win."

Chorus
Dogma has a fat power paw . . .
They are so uncouth.
Libra learns the truth.
Watching as they gnash and gnaw . . .
They even kill at will.
Libra learns the truth.

New ideas are what you need,
When you're not the one on top.
If we're going to succeed . . .
We've got to think outside the box.
He says with a malevolent grin,
"We'll do what it takes to win."

Chorus

11. Libra Met Her Match
(Chapter 12)
Amanda, Beatrice, and Mark Shelby, Johnny Freeman
Amsea Group, copyright 2002

Libra snuck into the Dogma meeting room . . .
And hid beneath a serving cart.
With all the ambiance of a pauper's tomb . . .
The meeting was about to start.

Pre-chorus 1
Hey! Catch that cat!
Where's it at?
I think it better scat! Yeah!

Chorus
Libra met her match.
Libra met her match.
Libra met her match.

Libra met her match.
Libra met her match.
Libra met her match . . . yeah

Up the air duct and to the roof . . .
Libra fin'ly gets away.
Down the outside wall she gently moves . . .
Trying to find a way to escape.

Pre-chorus 2
Oops! Libra didn't see!
Window opening!
Falling into trees! Yeah!

Chorus

Dogma found her communicator.
Heard Voca call Libra moments later.
They would track the signal to the ship.
Get the Marauders to go and destroy it.

Chorus (repeats)

12. Adele's Burden
(Chapter 13)
Amanda, Beatrice, and Mark Shelby, Johnny Freeman
Amsea Group, copyright 2002

"Stop that, Hank! See what you've done to the screen!"
He pulled back his paws and waited for breakfast.
Adele came out on the patio with a can of cat food.
Even though she had a sense of detachment mood.

Chorus
It's too heavy . . . it's too heavy!
The burden I must carry . . . now that he's gone.
Accident or murder.
Either way it hurts . . .
And it's too heavy . . . it's so hard to carry on.

Felix, my love, has been gone five months now.
Will I ever recover I don't know how.
Lost shipments, equipment failures, power outages
galore,
Quitting of senior scientists and so much more.

Chorus

Ohhh . . .

13. Invasion of the Marauders
(Chapter 14)
Amanda, Beatrice, and Mark Shelby, Johnny Freeman
Amsea Group, copyright 2002

A low muttering noise, growing louder by degrees.
Large black motorcycles came rumbling down the street.
Huge riders, pierced and tattooed from head to foot,
Crunched the grass, spewed the mountain air with soot.

Chorus
Hey! Hey! What's that sound?
The whirlybirds are flyin' around.
Hey! Hey! What's that sound?
Motorcycles are on the ground.

Ugly Marauder mood, brewing stronger by degrees,
Tossed on the meadow in the shade of the trees.
The riders pulled up near Voca's hiding place.
"Torch the place," said a man with an intimidating face.

Chorus

Pinny, the kitty, put out the fire with Voca's help.
A fire extinguisher brought out the pride in her.
Now she knows there are things she can do.
Just like me and you.

Chorus (repeats)

14. A Call To Cathy
(Chapter 15)
Amanda, Beatrice, and Mark Shelby, Johnny Freeman
Amsea Group, copyright 2002

The fall from the tall palm tree,
Really knocked the life right out of me.
Momma rat was quite a match.
Luckily, the grass was a safety catch.
A skate boarder rescued me.
Tucked me in her backpack, gently.
While she was skating along,
I awoke to remember what was wrong.

Chorus
I need to make a call to Cathy
Information please,
Los Gatos for Cathy Cameron, both names spelled with
"Cs."
I need to warn her of the danger.
Dogma will send a stranger.
I need to make a call to Cathy,
Information please.

Dogma Computer will strike,
Snuffing life in the fright of night.
Dogma killed Cathy's father and
Soon they'll be after the rest of them.
Now I have to contact her.
Gotta warn her of the danger.
The door's open at the cell phone store.
Finding a phone won't be a chore.

Chorus (repeats)

15. The Green Medallion
(Chapter 16)
Amanda, Beatrice, and Mark Shelby, Johnny Freeman
Amsea Group, copyright 2002

Hank and Piny, cats so tiny,
Showed acts of courage
Against an outrage
Of men so big and ugly
That had roared up, tored up, and burned up
The meadow where Voca was holed up.

Pre-chorus
Hank and Piny, cats so tiny
Deserve a reward.

Chorus
The Green Medallion,
Gatosian medal of honor.
The Green Medallion,
For acts of courage and valor.
Hank and Piny showed courage
In the face of danger
Battling the outrage
Of the Marauder's strangers
The Green Medallion...

Hank and Piny, cats so tiny
Brought down the riders
Doing some sliders
Into the poison ivy
That had grown up, shored up, and stung up
Anyone that got to be hung up.

Pre-chorus

Chorus

16. Born to Boogie
(Chapter 18)
Amanda, Beatrice and Mark Shelby
Amsea Group, copyright 2002

Tonight, I'm gonna tear up the town.
Nothing in this world to bring me down.
I feel so good; feel so right.
Can't wait to get on the floor tonight.
Watch out guys 'cause here I come.
Better get up and go, if you want some.

Chorus
Let's go do the desperado!
Follow up with the "Stray Cat."
We can even do the "Tahoe Twist."
I was born to boogie, born to boogie.

I'm asking for the next dance.
Won't you kindly give me a chance?
Let's get on the floor; do this right.
Show you how to have some fun tonight.
We punctuate every beat.
We'll turn the fire and feel the heat.

Chorus

17. Lunch at Aldo's
(Chapter 20)
Amanda, Beatrice, and Mark Shelby, Johnny Freeman
Amsea Group, copyright 2002

We need to talk scientifically,
Immediately,
And specifically about making a nanochip,
To repair the ship,
So Libra can get home again.

Chorus
We'll lunch at Aldo's,
Where the food is fine.
Fresh from the sea there's
Red lobster in wine.
We'll lunch at Aldo's.
Drink beer from a stein,
Watch the sunset and waste some time.

I'll show you all of the diagrams,
Replacement plans,
Along with all the parts needed to fix the ship,
Computer chips,
Using screechium catnip.

Chorus

18. Scrawny's Tree
(Chapter 21)
Amanda, Beatrice, and Mark Shelby, Johnny Freeman
Amsea Group, copyright 2002

Up a bumpy, curvy, windy road
Is an ancient redwood tree
Surrounded by dense new growth.
We can enter through its cavity.

Where sunlight filters down
Into the perfumed darkness all around.
The damp inner walls make us feel
Content and real.

Chorus
This tree lived through history,
Hundreds of years before you and me.
We call it . . . Scrawny's Tree.
It survived a lightning fire and logging gangs,
Hollowed out before axes rang.
We call it . . . we call it . . . Scrawny's Tree.

In the center circle moving ground
Is a bubble rising fast.
With stainless steel and clear plastic,
It's an elevator metallic shaft.

That plunges way down deep,
Into a lab with top secrets to keep.
We're standing in the back door.
Giant entrance to more.

Chorus

I see the branches of Scrawny's Tree,
Reaching up so majestically.
If a cat goes to heaven, it may be
On Scrawny's Tree.

Chorus

19. The Guardian
(Chapter 22)
Amanda, Beatrice, and Mark Shelby
Amsea Group, copyright 2002

Chorus
In the forest, the quiet forest,
The lion roars today.
Guardian of these mountains high,
Where the earth touches the sky.

Hank took a walk for fun,
In the warm morning sun.
Stopped totake a look around.

Full of curiosity,
Heard a noise suddenly.
Thought it was a vocal sound.

Hank had to check it out,
Wondering what it's all about,
Acting like a bloodhound.

Couldn't help but take a look
Following a babbling brook,
With his nose to the ground.

Chorus

Up the hill through the woods,
Anywhere the brook would,
Wondering where it ended at.

Spring flowing from the ground,
By an ancient redwood downed,
On the stump a giant cat.

I'm the guardian you see.
Here there is no trespassing.
Don't you know where you're at?

Hank put his mind at ease.
Told him that "I come in peace."
Hope that you're okay with that.

Chorus (repeats)

20. Altaperro
(Chapter 23)
Amanda, Beatrice and Mark Shelby, Johnny Freeman
Amsea Group, copyright 2002

Altaperro
Up a winding and narrow road,
With video cameras and sentry dogs,
Is an evil edifice above the smog.
In the shape of lower pit bulls' teeth,
With Alum Rock Park beneath.
It's not the jewel of San Jose,
That overlooks the yellowish brown haze.

Pre-chorus
It's Dogma's Altaperro,
Bastion of sorrow
For computer competitors,
Banks and creditors.

Chorus
Altaperro, Altaperro
Nothing's on the straight and narrow.
Adorned with gargoyles of greed,
Gnash and gnaw is your business creed.

Altaperro
Marble, steel, and bulletproof glass,
With bright monitors and guards in uniforms.
Looks like a country club of prison cell dorms,
With pit bulls meaner than junkyard dogs,
Leading riders on their hogs.
Looking for something they can slay.
They can't wait to gnash and gnaw away.

Pre-chorus

Chorus

Altaperro
Can our heroes get inside?
Will skunk oil spray with its noble bouquet,
Send those hungry sentry bloodhounds astray?
Will their nine-lives ray-o-vacs,
Be able to illuminate the facts?

Pre-chorus

Chorus

21. Screechium
(Chapter 24)
Amanda, Beatrice, and Mark Shelby, Johnny Freeman
Amsea Group, copyright 2002

In the lab below Scrawny's tree
Scientists were working diligently
To reconfigure the accelerator
They were pondering, then wondering,
Theoretical underpinnings,
Yarn theory, mew-ons, branched space-time
Black holes, white holes, gas holes to rhyme
Unified field theory, a favorite of mine.

Chorus
Screechium, screechium
A name that sounds like fingernails
Scraping on a chalkboard
An anti-matter element
Screechium, screechium
For the superconducting mew-on matrix
Used in the nano-chip for Libra's spaceship.

Implausible understandings.
Dark matter, bark-offs, worm hole ways,
Hot light, cold light, no light heat rays,
Energy from plasma, no distortion delays.

Chorus

Hold the matter, so it won't splatter
In the magnetic containment field.
Direct its flow to increase its yield
Into the matrix shield.

Chorus

22. Return of the Marauders
(Chapter 25)
Amanda, Beatrice, and Mark Shelby, Johnny Freeman
Amsea Group, copyright 2002

A low muttering noise growing louder by degrees,
Large black Harley hogs come rumbling through the
trees.
Each rider holds an iron pipe and handgun
Poised to kill man or creature just for fun.

Chorus
Uh! Oh! There's that sound!
The whirlybirds are flyin' around.
Uh! Oh! There's that sound!
Motorcycles are on the ground.

Pinny, Hand, and Voca really shaking where they stood,
Hank said he'd divert the riders to the woods.
Down the ramp Hank leaped, hitting the ground on the
run.
Crouched down low, he heard shots fired from a
Marauder's gun.

Chorus

Hanky, the kitty, led the riders from Libra's ship.
A dire emergency brought out the best in him.
Inner courage told him what to do,
Just like me and you.

Chorus (repeats)

23. Voca Rises
(Chapter 26)
Amanda, Beatrice, and Mark Shelby, Johnny Freeman
Amsea Group, copyright 2002

Now Voca has a new nanochip
To power Libra's spaceship.
He can fly to Altaperro
and try to save our heroes.
First, he'll sweep over the meadow
And take care of the Marauder fellows.

Chorus
Voca rises to the 'ccasion
With some crystal-blue persuasion.
The helicopters are down.
Now for the men on the ground!
Voca rises.

The Marauders are by the trees—
De-animator ray, please.
We'll give 'em all the best night's sleep.
Hold 'em for the law to keep.
Now we'll fly to Altaperro,
Where there's nothing on the straight and narrow.

Chorus

(Instrumental)

Chorus (repeats)

Voca rises, Voca rises, Voca rises, Voca rises

24. Pinny, You Can Fly
(Chapter 27)
Amanda, Beatrice, and Mark Shelby, Johnny Freeman
Amsea Group, copyright 2002

In Dogma's offices at Altaperro,
Cathy and Valdez make their way.
Their moving too easy, it's like play.
Squeaking on floors,
Opening doors, searching through drawers.
Then Trammel turns on the lights
And says, "Don't you know
Curiosity killed the cat?"

Chorus
Wham! Bam! Thank you, ma'am!
You just saved my life.
Pinny, you can fly!
You can fly in a cat's eye,
You just got the bad guy.
Pinny, you can fly!

In Trammel's offices at Altaperro
We're about to lose our heroes,
When Pinny and Libra fly inside,
Knocking Trammel over,
Like a boulder on his shoulder.
Then Valdez kicks Jug's gun
Out of his right hand
Just in time for Voca to land.

Chorus

The police have arrived at Altaperro
Where nothing's on the straight and narrow.
Trammel, Maraud, Debbitz, and others,
Will live in California prison cells,
With plenty of whistles and no bells.

Chorus (repeats)

25. Bye, Bye, Bye
(Chapter 28)
*Amanda, Beatrice and Mark Shelby, Johnny Freeman
Amsea Group, copyright 2002*

Now you've got your nanochip.
You can fly home in your spaceship.
You've made friends of man and cats.
You saved Silicon Valley from the Dogma rats.

Chorus
Bye, bye, bye, I'll try not to cry.
Though we'll never meet again.
Bye, bye, bye, I'll try not to cry.
It' so sad your stay must end.

We've learned that we're not alone.
Now it's time for you to go back home.
Your star shines through space and time.
Guided you here to explore this world of mine.

Chorus

It could be such a purr-fect world.
Like catnip euphoria.
Listening to the yarns you spin.
We really do adore ya!

Chorus